Margaret and Randy

Margaret and Randy

Margaret and Randy

Also by R. L. Rhyse

Margaret of Greenwich - Margaret and Erika

Margaret at War - Margaret in Tokyo

Margaret and Eve - Margaret and Velda

Margaret and Emily - Margaret and Hillary

Margaret in London - Margaret at Barnard

Margaret at Barnard/Part Two: Deliverance

Margaret in Berlin - Margaret in Manhattan

Margaret and Venla – Margaret: Mother of Twins - Margaret in Moscow

R. L. Rhyse

Margaret and Randy
Book Seventeen in the
Margaret of Greenwich® Series

Wyston Books, Inc.

Margaret and Randy

Wyston Books, Inc. – Warwick, New York

www.magaretofgreenwich.com

www.wystonbooks.com

Margaret and Randy: a novel

Book Seventeen in the Margaret of Greenwich® Series

1. Margaret of Greenwich (Fictitious character)
2. Teenage Girls Fiction
Library of Congress Control Number: 2020942434
ISBN 978-0-9991057-6-4
eISBN 978-0-9991057-9-5
Cover Photograph by Simon Potter/Cultura - Licensed from Getty Images
BISAC: YAF022000 (Girls & Women)
YAF011000 (Coming of Age)
YAF029000 (Law & Crime)

Margaret and Randy

Every friend's success is a triumph for all, showing that we can beat the odds.

—Margaret

Margaret and Randy

Introduction

"Be optimistic. You had an unforgettable wedding," Erika said a week later.

"The only thing worse would have been food poisoning," I said, morosely.

"Ouch. Even so, you're finally married though the groom did look faint," Erika said.

"Randy's a nervous guy," I said, lapsing into silence.

"To switch to a cheerier subject, did you hear the story that Jared told?"

"Which one?"

Jared, my distant cousin from Utah, makes a point of being outrageous at gatherings, being the colorful black sheep of my conservative Mormon clan.

"The one explaining why he'll always be afraid to marry."

"I can't wait."

"It went like this. He met this woman at the library."

"It was in a bar. He probably hasn't been in a library since grade school," I said, snappishly.

"That doesn't matter. After chatting her up, they wound up in bed."

"Knowing Jared, it doesn't surprise me."

Margaret and Randy

"Please!"

"Okay, I'll shut up."

"Once under the covers, he kisses her, moves his hand, and feels a very hairy leg. "What's this?" he asked. "That's my dog. I always sleep with him," the woman said. Jared gave her an ultimatum: "You either sleep with him or you sleep with me. You don't sleep with both!"

I waited expectantly. It was a good story but Erika had dragged out the suspense, being annoyed by my interruption.

"Well?" I finally asked.

"Jared went home."

"That must have deflated him, and taught him a lesson too," I said.

"Which is?"

"That things don't always work out as you expected," I said.

"It was certainly true of your wedding," Erika said.

And of this, *none* would argue against!

Chapter 1

Being married was different than I expected. Not being the Hollywood medley or fictional drama but just different. This might have been because we were already parents when tying the knot or both were consumed with our careers. Or maybe we had simply known each other too long.

Randy entered my life about the time of my first period though this never became a topic of our conversation. Nor is it with most husbands, even those less frightened of the sight of blood than him.

Despite his intellect, Doctor Randy (his doctorate is in computer science) remains a worry-wart. Getting him vaccinated is gained by the presence of our children. Then, wanting to set a good example, he manages to smile during the procedure. But kids are perceptive and I'm not sure they're convinced. Though only four, *they* no longer need hand-holding during vaccination.

Some say that the barometer of a couple's happiness is how often they have sex. If so, ours is low or maybe it's me. Not that Randy is *never* passionate but not often. Was our sex ever more frequent, you ask? Yes, soon after our first time when I was eighteen. Which is old in today's culture and considering how long we had dated before.

Not that we didn't want sex but emotions interfered. Some from my Mormon upbringing which frowns on pre-marital sex and some from his fear of feelings which has always been an issue. But maybe our biggest problem, though I hate to admit it, is mine and inevitable.

Margaret and Randy

Perhaps like every genius, Randy needs someone to manage his life: to care for his children, arrange his schedule, buy his clothes and more. And while I'm sure he appreciates this, it also bothers him because ever since childhood he had fantasies of being a Navy SEAL. Who, at least according to their public image, *don't* need a woman to care for them!

Chapter 2

Despite my complaints, the good thing about being married is that Randy lives with us. Earlier, while a graduate student, he lived in an apartment near school. Now he's home most of the time except when at a professional conference or hustling a business idea. But these can last for weeks and cause our toddlers to call him their "flying daddy."

I can't brush this off as easily, tending to worry about the desirable women he must meet while traveling, all more fascinating than the harried mother that he's married to.

Sadly, this issue couldn't be talked about considering Randy's minimal communication skills. Raising it would have led to the non-discussions we earlier had about whether to marry since neither love nor attraction can be forced as everyone knows. Thus we carried on: loving our kids; performing dutiful sex; and busily working in markedly different careers.

Decision nodes, where critical events hang in the balance, are like the railway switching yards of history when the smallest change can send a train laden with armies in a totally different direction. Changes then branch exponentially from rails to streets to families. Which is how our nightmare began: with an accident on our wedding day and Randy screaming, "It wasn't my fault!"

A girl of about ten lay on the sidewalk beside her bike as Randy stood beside his car, an old Ford Thunderbird two-seater gifted by his father. Like most moms I drove an SUV but he still hadn't come to grips with being a parent. *Someday* he will, I had been telling myself.

Margaret and Randy

Randy is high strung, as evidenced by his unjustified guilt at the accident. I rushed to the girl and bent low to speak.

"Are you alright?" I asked

I reached to help her up but she resisted, seeming to prefer staying where she was. My toddlers wandered beside me and stared, like the rest of the wedding party and Randy who had recovered from his shock.

This silent tableau of adults, children, and prostrate girl persisted until she spoke in a foreign language which I recognized from my study in Berlin. My knowledge of German was poor so I didn't understand but Gerald, a wedding guest, spoke it fluently.

"What did she say?" I asked.

Gerald lifted and held the girl tightly before speaking, then gave me a strange look as if it were something he shrank from repeating.

"She said they weren't moving. That both were dead," he said.

Chapter 3

The impact of these words spread rapidly. Smiles disappeared from adults and children's play languished as they sensed anxiety and that something bad had happened. Being the hostess, I took charge of the remaining minutes of my reception. It can be impossible to revive a party that's gone flat but I tried.

"Please return to the house. There's plenty of food," I said loudly.

The guest list hadn't been large. Apart from family and friends, there were business associates of the billionaire father of my best friend, Erika, and investors in my husband's business. Bodyguards quickly surrounded their charges, shuffling them inside and away from windows.

Gerald, still grasping the girl, ordered me inside too. I grabbed my toddlers and obeyed as Sergeant Alamo of the Greenwich Police Department, a long-time family friend, grabbed his phone. As police cruisers and bedlam descended, I felt the unseemly gratitude that this interruption hadn't stopped our marriage, which Randy had avoided for years. Getting him to the altar again might never have happened.

Leaving my home now became as much a ceremony as the marital vows as the police took charge. Guests' names were taken and the bodyguards' weapons permits were checked. This took hours and it was nearly 6PM before the last guest left though immediate families remained to provide support.

Margaret and Randy

The girl, whose appearance had aroused this bedlam, sat mute with Gerald at her side. Connecticut's Department of Social Services had been notified and would take charge.

We waited and eventually received their phone call. There had been an apartment house fire in neighboring Stamford. A single parent died in it while her three children were at school. The Department couldn't immediately pick up my charge. A nurse would be over to check her vitals but could she stay with us for a few days? I said that she could and thus did Asya enter our lives.

Chapter 4

"Brides never get a new child on their wedding day. You're the first that I ever heard of but then your life was never typical," my mother said the next day.

This was another certainty since my birth. Even now when atypical families units are common, mine is extraordinary since I have *three* fathers and *three* mothers. Okay, like all species only one of each is my biological relative but I love them all and they love me, which is what really counts isn't it?

Now to clarify this inescapable confusion. My biological mother gave me up for adoption at birth and I was raised by adoptive parents. At the time of my conception, my mother had simultaneous affairs with two men: a retired Russian general who managed an international security company in Germany, and a British spy living in Brussels.

Thus do I have a biological mother, an adoptive mother, and my Berlin father's live-in girlfriend as stepmother. I am considered their children's aunt and my children are considered their cousins. Asya's status, as I told my children, was as "our guest."

Having to cope with trauma as Asya was doing wasn't new in my circle. My best friend, Erika's, mother had been murdered when she was a child and her step-sister was rescued from a sex-trafficking ring. But that Asya spoke German presented an additional problem since mine was far from fluent. Thus to all my maternal tasks was added the English language instruction of this ten-year-old girl.

Chapter 5

Though international adoptions are frequent, language is not usually a problem since the child is either an infant or one who already speaks their new family's language. But lacking English wasn't Asya's only adjustment difficulty, the effect of her trauma being far greater.

The public agencies helped as best they could. Her interviews were few and unhelpful. Asya had been in a closet, hiding from a nightmare-induced monster, when the murders occurred so she knew little about them. Her other information, that she was the only child of a German diplomat's family, complicated matters further with America's State Department becoming involved.

None of which made a difference to our family. We accepted her presence whole-heartedly as did the entire community. Her tragedy energized Greenwich with offers of aid and adoption pouring in.

It was like what happens when a child falls into a well or is lost in the forest and attention focuses on them as opposed to larger problems, perhaps feeling that it is more manageable. But interest in the murders diminished as nothing new was reported and the public quickly turned to other matters.

Meanwhile, life in our family continued. Married life was new for me and my toddlers since their father had not earlier lived with us continuously. Asya's presence was an added stress though none of us minded. The government psychologist who evaluated her considered her best treatment to be a normal home life which we tried to provide.

Margaret and Randy

I told my four-year-old twins that Asya had a bad experience and they should help her. Which they did by offering her toys and, despite the language difference, trying to engage her in play. Though behaving robotically, Asya recognized their desire and let them play around her which they accepted. Children can sense another's pain.

Chapter 6

Before marrying, my household consisted of: my four-year-old twins; James and Donna; our family bodyguard, Mila, who also acted as emergency babysitter; their regular sitter/high school student, Maria, and her mother, Annette, who cleaned my home and downtown office. Her young son sometimes accompanied her and was a playmate for my children.

In addition to my household duties, I managed the East Coast office of a security company servicing the rich, famous, and government employees who were neither. Thus two bedrooms in my large home were reserved for clients that needed secure emergency housing, usually before leaving the country. At those times, another bodyguard would stay over.

Apart from these peculiarities ours was a normal home. Or as typical as any containing two steel-lined security rooms with an independent telephone line, air supply system and electrical service, a porta-potty, and weapons. More of these measures exist than you might think.

The presence of young children bring many tasks. The need to do laundry increases exponentially and friends pop in without warning for a Mother's Respite (called a Playdate) during which refreshments and adult conversation are expected. Meanwhile, business demands can occur anytime for a mother juggling her career even while coping with their child's illness.

That James' illness wasn't serious didn't keep me from worrying which is every mother's preoccupation. But Mila's words reassured me. Before being employed by my company

Margaret and Randy

as a bodyguard, she had been a medical doctor in Russia's Special Forces.

"A hundred-degree fever isn't critical in a child particularly since he's not complaining. If it rises, you'll see the pediatrician. Until then, stop worrying and get back to work. I'll watch him."

Then *the* phone call came.

Chapter 7

"Where *exactly* is your house?" the voice asked, in a clipped English accent.

It was the mildly familiar voice of an older man. Certainly not of a door-to-door salesman in my tony Greenwich neighborhood. Nor would a stranger have my cell phone number.

Momentarily forgetting my worry about James, I asked, "Who is this?"

During the delay before answering, I heard the rustle of the phone being handed over and recognized the next voice immediately.

"Darling, we're lost," my English grandmother said, in a mock plaintive tone.

"Huh?"

This juvenile expression, which I had long tried to rid myself of, burst out.

"Victoria?" I asked, astonished.

"Am I not welcome?"

"You're *always* welcome but where are you?"

"We just passed an Apple store. The sign said Greenwich Avenue."

Margaret and Randy

"You're in *Greenwich*?" I asked, still feeling dazed.

"*Darling...*" Victoria said, drawling as only the upper-class English can.

"I'm still surprised but overjoyed. I never needed you as much as I do now," I said, fervently.

This wasn't wholly true but every mother needs her understanding mother sometimes and a grandmother understands life even better. Grandmother Victoria would have a different take on events, having been being brought up in an earlier age amidst rigidly class-conscious England. As a youth she had been a debutante at Buckingham Palace. I expected that the man with her was her combination driver-bodyguard, Mr. Jenkins.

She passed back the phone and I gave him directions. They would arrive in minutes and I went to primp myself. During my summer in London I learned that her concept of acceptable dress differed greatly from mine.

Being in the business, my home security system was state-of-the-art. It would surprise Grandmother Victoria and impress Mr. Jenkins.

Chapter 8

My security system *did* shock them. Picture a robotic, human voice asking your identity. Not expecting anyone else, I immediately buzzed them in though Mila would have objected. She meets visitors at the door with readied pistol.

Grandmother Victoria is the oldest relative of my atypical family. Always faultlessly dressed and inherently polite, she seems to belong to another time and does. Picture the scene as the wise mistress of Downton Abbey visiting her rougher, less organized granddaughter and grandchildren and you won't be far wrong.

Mr. Jenkins, a retired Scotland Yard detective, had worked for Victoria so long as to be almost a member of the family. Which is how I considered him but he did not. Upper-class English are formal about such things so while Victoria and I chatted of family matters, Mila and he shared their movie-worthy life experiences.

"How are you?" Victoria asked, with a penetrating gaze.

"Now that we're married?" I asked indirectly, with words that were an answer in itself.

Victoria waited silently.

"I'm disappointed," I said honestly.

Again she waited silently until I spoke.

Margaret and Randy

"I'm glad that we're finally married, both for myself and the children. They needed a live-in father but still don't have one. Randy is obsessed with his work and away for weeks at a time. He's developed a reputation in cybersecurity which is now a hot field. I almost wish that he'd accept one of the many government jobs he's been offered, one with regular hours and free weekends. But I also know that he'd be miserable and maybe take it out on us."

Her next question shocked me. It wouldn't if coming from a friend but she was of an entirely different generation. Still, since she's the mother of a renowned British spy, I shouldn't have been surprised.

"How often do you have sex?" she asked.

Chapter 9

In these free-wheeling times when celebrity woes are publicly discussed, I shouldn't have been shocked by Victoria's question but was. Had my best friend asked it I would have answered without pause but wouldn't from a mother and particularly a grandmother. It was as if they *never* had sex which I knew was nonsense. Victoria lessened my embarrassment.

"I've surprised you," she said.

"Yes, you did. I've come to believe that the English worship form with sex not being spoken of and considered to be reserved for marriage," I said honestly, directness being my style.

"You're partly correct. In my time there were frequent weekend parties where couples paired off, allegedly unseen but certainly whispered about, My faithfulness to your grandfather was the exception. But you haven't answered my question which was asked not from prurience but from concern. All factors being equal, a couple's happiness can be measured by how often they have sex. The less frequent as compared to when it was most frequent, the bigger are their problems. It's a simple equation."

What she said made such good sense that I answered immediately.

Margaret and Randy

"We haven't had sex for weeks. Before giving birth, at its most frequent, we'd spend all day in bed. Becoming parents made a difference. I'm easily distracted with worry about the kids. Donna once popped into our room when... I can't imagine what she thought."

"Kids are sturdy. She'll survive," Victoria said, supportively.

"What do you advise?" I asked.

"That's something you'll have to work out by yourselves. A marriage is like a sailor traveling the sea: being a means to an end which here is a comforting life. Events are usually benign but can rarely be lethal and the risk never goes away."

A rustling in the doorway interrupted our conversation. Following the psychologist's advice, we had allowed Asya to wander freely about the house and she stood listening.

"Come in, Asya. I'll introduce you to Grandmother Victoria," I said, in my hesitant German.

Chapter 10

Asya stood paralyzed, looking like a discovered, cornered animal.

"It's all right, Asya. Grandma Victoria loves children. She has a grown-up boy," I said.

I extended my hand and Asya approached. Holding her against me, I said, "Grandma Victoria, this is Asya. She's living with us for a while."

To my surprise, Victoria reached out and, touching Asya's hand, spoke in German.

"My dear child, you've had a hard time. I hope we can be friends."

It might have Victoria's greater German fluency than mine or something in her tone but Asya responded, speaking more than since she had arrived bloodied at our doorstep. Recognition flickered in her eyes and her phrasing was more formal than one would expect of a ten-year-old. She's had good parenting, I thought.

"I'm pleased to meet you. Are you visiting America from Germany?" she asked.

This logical question might indicate that she's coming out of her fugue state and could provide information. The police should be told, I thought.

Margaret and Randy

"No. I've just arrived from London to visit my daughter and grandchildren. Have you met them?" Victoria asked, slowly.

I recognized her attempt to keep the conversation innocent, far from the jarring events that triggered Asya's arrival.

"Yes, James and Donna. They've shared their toys though they are too young for me."

"You're a big girl," Victoria said.

"I am, and have been promised a phone," Asya said.

"Then we must shop for your phone. Do you like to go shopping?" Victoria asked.

"Yes, but I'm not allowed to now. Will you take me?"

"If Margaret says it's alright. Margaret, would you allow Asya to go shopping with me?" Victoria asked, turning toward me.

"That would be fine. Perhaps you can go tomorrow," I said.

Preparations need be made. In view of the recent events, I wanted them accompanied by *two* bodyguards and traveling in the armored SUV which was my latest company perk.

Asya slumped against me, as if the lengthy conversation had tired her. Victoria noticed this too.

Margaret and Randy

"We can talk more later. Would you like to have a nap?" Victoria asked.

Asya nodded and slowly disengaged from me. Victoria accompanied her upstairs.

"I didn't know you spoke German," I said, when Victoria returned.

"My dear, there's much about me that you don't know," Victoria said, though kindly and with twinkling eyes.

I let that pass without comment.

"Asya is a Russian name. It's an unusual name to be given a German child since Germans tend to be traditional," Victoria said.

I stared at her for a moment. Her comment had been calculated.

"Asya is the nickname for Anastasia," she said.

Margaret and Randy

Chapter 11

"Children don't put as much energy into being sad as adults but Asya is mourning," Victoria said.

"I would expect so," I said.

"The news reports were fragmentary and soon disappeared. What actually happened at her home?" Victoria asked.

"Her parents were killed," I said.

"And?"

"They were tortured. It isn't known why," I said.

"For money? Drugs?"

"He was Germany's Consul-General in Manhattan and their money came from his salary. There is no indication that he used drugs or dealt them."

"They were tortured for information," Victoria asserted.

"That's the logical conclusion and what the police are working on."

"Could it be a military secret?" Victoria asked.

Margaret and Randy

"According to our company's intelligence, Germany's military is in such disarray that it has none worth stealing. That may be an exaggeration but..."

"Do they have other children?" Victoria asked.

"No. The wife couldn't conceive even with treatments. She had two miscarriages and they'd given up, the investigator said."

"Asya was their only child," Victoria mused.

"That's the biggest mystery. She never was their child," I said.

I had learned during my teenage summer in London that the British don't cotton to emotions and what produces laughter among Americans *might* arouse their chuckle. Victoria's raised eyebrows revealed that my information had startled her.

"They never had children," she said, slowly.

"No."

"Then whose child is Asya and how did she get here?"

"That, as Americans say, is the sixty-four-dollar question. There is no record of Asya's adoption in Germany or entering this country. As far as the two governments are concerned, she doesn't exist," I said.

"Asya doesn't exist," Victoria repeated.

"Except that she's been living in Greenwich," I said.

Margaret and Randy

A silence followed until Victoria spoke.

"She told me a secret."

"What?" I asked.

"That she's called *Princess*," Victoria revealed.

Chapter 12

When considering my recent marriage, Asya's shocking arrival and my English grandmother's visit, one would expect that fate had placed more than enough on my plate but it wasn't so. My friend, Erika, with whom I had long been as close as a sister, was in the final stage of pregnancy and greatly needed me. She had empathized throughout my pregnancy and now I had to be there for her.

"When?" I asked, as she exhaustedly fell onto the sofa.

"My due date is next month," Erika said.

"Don't be moralistic about accepting an epidaual," I advised, with concern.

"You didn't have one."

"I didn't need it. The kids popped out. I nearly set a record for delivery."

"Maybe I'll break it. How's your latest addition doing?" she asked.

"I don't know. She's out shopping with Victoria and seems okay but I can't understand how. To hear your parents being tortured and murdered must affect you but after her first days here she seemed almost normal."

"Almost?"

Margaret and Randy

"Her older behavior is understandable since she was an only child but she also has a dignity that I've never seen in one so young. Maybe that's why she cottons to Victoria, both considering themselves to be of a higher class."

"Victoria is exceptionally courteous to everyone regardless of their station in life," Erika said.

"That's an English upper-class thing."

"How do your kids relate to Asya?"

"Very well, It's as if they sense her hurt and are trying to help her," I said.

"What about Randy?"

"The same, when he's home."

"He still travels a lot?"

"Still," I said, wearily.

This was my frequent complaint.

Chapter 13

Neither of us spoke for a long while but it was a comfortable silence. One that develops between trusted friends when words aren't needed.

"Have you and Clarence set the date?" I asked.

Greenwich is a historically conventional town and unmarried parents are rare among the majority prosperous families. I was the first of our circle but Erika would be the more notable since her father was one of the town's billionaires.

"Nerds fear commitment lest it crimp their creativity," Erika said.

"Clarence can't believe that! He's much too smart," I insisted.

"Maybe not or it could be his diabetes," she said.

"Diabetics never marry?" I asked.

"Being diagnosed with diabetes changed him. Before, getting sick was simply something that he got over. Now he needs continual reassurance. It's good his doctor understands him," Erika said.

"What does being diabetic have to do with marrying?" I persisted.

"He's afraid he'll leave me a young widow."

Margaret and Randy

Another apparently irresolvable family problem, I told myself, as silence ensued.

"Does your security company deal with personal issues?" Erika asked, suddenly.

"That's most of our business, Only twenty-percent is government work," I said.

"And it's *confidential?* You can't talk about it?" she asked, sheepishly.

I took a moment before answering. Asking if we kept confidences is like asking a mother if she'd sell her child. But I restrained my hurt, knowing that many security companies aren't as ethical as ours.

"Do you really feel the need to ask?" I said softly.

"No, of course not. I'm not thinking clearly. It's a sensitive matter," Erika said, slowly.

"OK," I said, letting the increasing silence pressure her revelation.

"You employ former military?" Erika asked.

"They're most of our staff," I said.

A thoughtful expression settled on Erika's face. She's wondering how much to reveal, I told myself.

"Does your company have employees who kill?" she asked.

Margaret and Randy

I looked closely. Erika was serious.

Chapter 14

Words are like arrows shot into the sky. If falling harmlessly onto a field they have no destructive effect. But if striking a person, big worry starts.

Thus one who speaks of wanting to have a person killed is either crazy or seriously upset. Now Erika definitely wasn't crazy since she had many years of therapy. She was also very smart. Not in a school sense like my Randy or her Clarence but being intuitively clever. Able to see practical solutions while others are still scratching their head. So she wasn't joking and I took her question seriously. But, being the daughter of a lawyer, I also knew what should never be said.

"We're not murderers even if our government sanctioned work has involved killing criminals to save lives. Words matter so we must speak carefully. I believe what you're saying is that an unbelievably bad person has made you fear for your safety. Wouldn't this be more accurate?" I asked, speaking slowly to emphasize my words.

"Yes, exactly. I misspoke," Erika said, having regained self-control.

"My company specializes in these situations and has never lost a client. We do whatever is needed to assure their safety," I said.

Margaret and Randy

I gripped her hand so she would grasp my unsaid meaning: that I would do *anything* to protect her. Her family was as mine and one doesn't desert their family.

"Thank you. I have no one else," Erika said.

This statement surprised me since she was close with her family.

Grasping my quizzical look, Erika said, "Not with this. No one must learn of it."

"I can't help you without knowing everything," I said.

"You'll think me an idiot. Must you?" she asked, with pleading eyes, though knowing the answer.

"Nothing that you've done or will do can make me think less of you," I said emphatically, tightening my grip on her hand.

Her story flowed as if from a bursting dam and when she finished I wanted to kill too.

Chapter 15

"Clive was older, a graduate student that I met in the college library. We had the school in common but nothing else. He was adopted as a child, sent from heroin addicted parents to a wealthy family. He was smart, had graduated from Phillips Exeter and was admitted to three Ivy League colleges before deciding on Yale.

"It was a bad time in my life. Clarence was consumed with his studies and had little time for me, my dad was involved with his work and new wife and I felt alone."

"There was always me," I said, softly.

"Yes, but you were pregnant and had troubles with Randy and your job."

"Your problem is from a past relationship?" I asked, trying to speed her story along.

"Yes and no since our affair didn't last. He graduated and drifted off and I tried to forget him. This wasn't hard since I didn't love him and our relationship betrayed what I want with Clarence: that there be no secrets and certainly no lovers. I'm positive he hasn't had any."

"It'll take time. The mind has its own schedule for forgetting and caring for your baby will wipe out other concerns," I said supportively.

"Ordinarily. That's how it would have been until Clive re-entered my life."

"You slept with him again?" I asked.

"Of course not! Like this?" Erika asked, touching her swollen belly and exhibiting her first smile since we met that day.

"So what happened?" I asked.

"Ten-thousand-dollars a month is what happened. Unless I pay, he'll spread the video of our sexcapade across the internet. It was taken with a hidden camera and I had no idea."

"Why not tell the police about this blackmail?" I asked.

"'Because publicity can destroy. I help manage my dad's hedge fund. Consider the video's effect on that and Clarence and my family. And what's on the Internet lasts forever. Would you want your kids seeing you in such a thing when they grow up?" Erika asked.

"You want him out of your life and the film to disappear," I summarized.

"At whatever cost," Erika said fervently.

Silence filled the room as I thought. Despite being multi-national, ours is a small company. When a specialist is needed, we out-source using the contacts of our Directors who are former officials of the CIA, British Secret Service, or Russian military. My office consisted of just me, my assistant,

Margaret and Randy

Jordan, a West Point graduate, and his wife. Elizabeth, who helped with paper work Coping with a blackmailer required an agent who was seventy-percent thug, twenty-percent crook, and the rest goodness of heart, But though needing help, I also knew where to get it.

"Your family employs our company for security so we'll consider this as part of our service. You'll only be charged for unusual expenses. If you're tight because of the baby and all, I'll cover it," I said.

"Bless you! I was so worried," Erika burst out, and began sobbing.

"We're family," I said, simply.

Chapter 16

Though my promise to Erika was easily made, I needed help to accomplish it. Over an encrypted line, I phoned my father/corporate boss, Vladimir, in Berlin, described her problem and what I required.

"I need one or two English speaking agents as quickly as possible. They should be seventy-percent thug, twenty-percent crook, and the rest goodness of heart. Do we have them?" I asked.

After momentary deliberation came his welcome reply, "I can get them."

I let out the breath that I'd been holding.

"Send them on a private plane so they can leave the country quickly afterward," I said.

"Good thinking, They'll arrive tomorrow night. Keep me informed," Vladimir said.

I wasn't unfamiliar with blackmail, having once extracted a doctor from a similar situation. The only certainty in meeting a blackmailer's demand is that they'll return for more if their victim pays.

The officially advised way to deal with them is through the court but for prominent people this is a losing game. Even if the criminal is jailed, their reputation will become saddled with a lifetime stain in this internet age.

Margaret and Randy

While I had told Erika that our company didn't kill for hire, our unofficial maxim is that there is a justice of the lawyer and the courtroom and a justice of The Prophets and of God. After musing this, I put the matter out of mind. Nothing could be done until the agents arrived and worrying would interfere with the critical thinking that was needed to solve Erika's problem.

I checked in on James who was busily playing Candy Land with Mila.

"I'm winning!" he proudly exclaimed.

Mila feigned sobbing to James' delight and, when he dozed, I took her aside.

"Two agents will arrive tomorrow, using the north bedrooms for a few days. The children shouldn't see them. They were never here," I said pointedly.

My instruction didn't need elaboration. Mila, a former agent, knew the score.

Chapter 17

"You're perkier," I told Erika when we met the next morning.

"Because I'm no longer alone," she said.

"You never were. Feeling ashamed clouds the mind. We'll do our best," I said.

"That's good enough for me. Whatever problem you put your mind to, you manage to fix on your terms," she said.

"I try," I said, feeling humbled by her praise.

" I haven't heard from Clive in a week. Maybe he's had second thoughts about blackmail," Erika said, hopefully.

"No, he's being clever. Uncertainty creates anxiety and weakness in the target. You'll hear from him," I said.

"Should I do anything now?" Erika asked.

"Just relax and leave the worrying to our company. Your big day will soon be here. Do you have a name for your son?" I asked.

"His father was bullied in school because of his name. He doesn't care so long as it's common and won't invite it. I'm torn between Jack and Clark."

"What do your parents think?" I asked.

Margaret and Randy

"They haven't said a word, being involved with my stepmother's pregnancy. The house will soon be awash in babies," Erika said.

"Until you get your own house."

"Maybe it's our generation but I like living at home. Not after Clarence and I marry, but for now it's secure and easy," Erika said.

"It's good that you're happy," I said.

Further comment would be grouchy. Erika's family home was a forty-million-dollar mansion and with domestic help. Having live-in bodyguards, multiple alarm systems and a steel-lined security room on each floor made it as safe as the White House.

"Any more advice before I enter motherhood?" she asked.

Is there? I·asked myself. Erika had attended nearly all my medical exams and mothering classes and been present in the delivery room. What more need she know?

"Yes, something that took me a while to learn: how much words can both hurt and heal. When your child is being impossible, don't let the anger you express be unequal to the aggravation. Raging at a child inflicts hurt and in our heart we know that the old saying, 'Sticks and stones can break my bones but words will never harm me,' isn't true," I said.

"That's impressive advice," Erika said.

Margaret and Randy

"It's not mine. I read it in a book by a rabbi, *Words That Hurt, Words That Heal.* I'll buy it for you. He's an artist," I said.

"Art is the gift that God gave us to solve problems in a merciful way. Maybe even mine," she said, hopefully.

Chapter 18

"Still renovating?" I asked.

Since we first met, Erika had re-decorated her bedroom every year. When her father complained of the cost, she replied, "It's cheaper than using drugs," which shut him up. He always gave her what she wanted, feeling guilty because of her mother's killing by a business rival who then attempted Erika's murder.

"Sure, though not with anything precious since the rooms will shortly be filled with kids," Erika said.

"What's the latest?" I asked, seeking ideas for my home from her impeccable taste.

"My dad's architect created rooms with oppressive formality and far too much white. Kids love nooks to hide in and be alone. I added color to make it more flattering throughout the day. White looks dingy in many light conditions," she said.

"You want to maintain a home's grandeur without letting the décor be overblown, respecting its roots," I said.

"That's it! With the children's own library and playroom and a tween-size bed and upholstered head-and-footboard to fit the window nook when they grow into it. My stepmom suggested covering the short closet doors that flank the nook in Finnish wallpaper from Tapettitalo, making them almost invisible, and with a pierced brass Shadow Ball light based on a 17th century English design, riffs on the idea of a disco ball," Erika said.

My smile of delight became forced and Erika noticed.

"What's wrong?" she asked, with concern.

We were like blood-sisters, bound together in an often cob-webby world. Even then, it took several moments for me to speak.

"Growing up means seeing things as they are and taking them as they come. Those who don't can make a stiff pain of themselves," I said, and paused.

Erika nodded agreement and I continued.

"There's something that I want to ask. I intended never to because I know how hesitant you might be about replying but maybe you won't anymore. Do you know what I'm thinking?"

"Despite your tongue-tied way of putting it, I think I do,"

"And you won't mind my asking?"

"Try me."

"Do you think Randy *really* loves me?" I asked, uttering the question that I had dreaded speaking.

Chapter 19

Why did I ask *Erika* if Randy loved me? Psychologists call people like her *a hero*. Someone who always seems to know who they are and where they're going. A shining figure whom others look up to, but also because she knew me best. We had grown up together for more than half our lives and I trusted her judgment.

"Why do you ask that *now*?" she asked.

Answering my question with hers wasn't what I expected but I went along since she has great intuition. Though I didn't want to explain, as if speaking the words would make my concern more real. Still, as when one consults a doctor, they can't help unless you tell them everything so I did.

"I expected Randy to jump me when he got back but we haven't had sex for weeks. And it's not that I wasn't receptive or that the kids were disruptive since they've been sleeping fine.

"He's always been good with them but now when he plays with them he seems distracted. It could be a business problem and I know there's no normal frequency of having sex for a married couple but I do expect it more than once a month and that's in a good month. I mean, we're just barely not teenagers," I said.

Erika rolled her eyes and smiled.

Margaret and Randy

"Okay, nearer mid-twenties," I corrected.

"Honesty is the best policy. I've tried everything else," Erika said.

We both smiled.

"Have you noticed anything disturbing?" she asked.

I had read enough romance novels to know what she meant: finding lipstick on his collar, a woman's panty in his jacket pocket, or condoms in his wallet.

"Do instant phone hang-ups and calls that he goes into another room to take count?" I asked.

"Is there anything else?" Erika asked, into the silence that followed.

"There's Valerie," I said, with a sigh.

Chapter 20

"Valerie?" Erika asked.

"A computer nerd from Columbia who he bounces ideas off, he says."

"So?"

"So I saw her Facebook photos and can't help wondering what else he bounces off her."

Erika didn't reply, simply staring as one does when they sense that their best friend has gone off the rails.

"Are they naked in the pictures?" she asked rhetorically, trying to get me down to earth.

When I glared as response, she went on.

"Okay, tell me about Valerie."

"Cute. Blond hair, pink jacket, white blouse and scarf, truly short skirt. A real handful."

"You do have it though I never thought you would," Erika said.

"I have what?" I asked, my anxiety giving way to puzzlement.

"The uncertainty that everyone has after making a big decision. You've just married Randy after ten years of simply dating despite having two children together. It's fairly common that couples who marry after living together for a long time soon separate, marriage arousing too great the feeling of loss of identity through the merger. You might not feel this but could fear that he does and seeing Valerie's picture aroused your fear," Erika said.

And just like that, a moment after she finished speaking, my anxiety disappeared. Like after getting the negative result of a feared medical test or the pediatrician saying that your child's symptom isn't serious.

"You're right!" I said, placing my hand over hers.

"Don't mention it. That's what friends are for," Erika said, with a smile.

"I feel as if we're living our lives with one foot in a rose garden and the other in quicksand," I said.

"Like back in high school?" Erika asked.

We laughed before becoming serious again.

"In the depth of winter, I finally learned that within me there lay an invincible summer," she said.

"That's deep," I said.

"It should be. The French Nobel winner, Albert Camus, wrote it many years ago."

Chapter 21

Erika was calmer when she left and I felt relieved. The days preceding my childbirth weren't so distant that I couldn't empathize with what she was experiencing.

My toddlers napped and Victoria and Asya hadn't yet returned from shopping so I attended to business matters in my home office. There, things always buzzed from the latest terrorist alerts and financial scams which were of interest to the many corporations that we serviced.

One investor lost twenty-four-million-dollars in cryptocurrency when his phone was hacked despite all his security precautions. While working from his home in Las Vegas, someone in Connecticut had hijacked his phone. Then, after taking over his Gmail account using Google's "Forgot Password" feature, they reset it, locking him out and stealing from his cryptocurrency digital wallet. Thankfully, he wasn't one of our clients. Trying to explain *that* to my boss wouldn't be pleasant!

The phone rang as my eyes began glazing over.

"Can you and the children come for dinner tonight?" my mother asked.

"We'd love to," I said.

"Randy too if he's home," she said.

Margaret and Randy

"He's not back yet but the kids will love seeing you. You and dad are their favorites," I said.

"Ever since we spoiled them while you were in Russia."

"And because you're the best," I said sincerely.

"They can cheer up our dinner guest."

"Do I know him?" I asked.

"Judd Redmond, your dad's law partner before going to a huge law firm."

"What's he sad about?" I asked.

"He's getting a divorce and has job issues too."

"I thought the legal business was booming," I said.

"You'll get an earful tonight and maybe business," my mother said, cryptically.

"I'll dress to impress and the kids too," I said, and we both laughed.

I extended my mother's invitation to Victoria. She said that she would stay home with Asya, who had rarely left the house since arriving.

"Will we get presents?" James asked, excitedly, when he learned.

"Relatives don't always give bought presents. Love is the greatest present of all,"

Margaret and Randy

An important task of parenting is to push life-affirming maxims on your children.

Chapter 22

The children had napped in the afternoon so were wide awake when it was time to leave. Which didn't mean that they were ready since a child's schedule rarely accords with their parent's. Still, they did their best and getting dressed involved less hassle than usual. That their grandmother permitted them sweets may have been a factor. Sweets aren't considered food by their mother.

My parents' home is only a five-minute drive. This could create difficulties for other families but not mine. Each member lives their independent life with only a loving and not pathological dependence existing.

Though now having my own home, entering theirs was always a joy. I still experienced it as my *real* home, such is the influence of childhood.

Thanks to my toddlers, we arrived a few minutes late. In other families, guests would have awaited us holding alcoholic drinks but ours was a Mormon family. Not rigidly, for then I wouldn't have married outside my religion, but being respectful of the Mormon prohibition against consuming alcohol which I observed in my home too.

As the children scampered with this home's cache of their toys, the adults became acquainted. Judd was a short, stout, man in his fifties with long sideburns and a receding hairline. His girlfriend, Ada, was a little shorter, had flaming red hair, and looked to be in her thirties.

Margaret and Randy

"What beautiful children," she said, which caused me to like her immediately.

Judd's smile didn't reach his eyes. I sensed his tension and remembered my mother saying that my company might pick up business tonight. Maybe, maybe not, I thought, since we refuse divorce cases.

Chapter 23

I wanted to question my mother about what she had said but also to not leave my toddlers and that won out. I watched as they repeatedly placed checkers in the Connect Four game, then argued over who would noisily release the pieces onto the floor. Judd approached and I looked up.

"Your dad told me you manage a security company," he said.

"Yes, it's international," I said, not wanting him to think we supplied night watchmen.

"What does it do?" he asked, opening the way for my sales pitch.

"Our main office is in Berlin with subsidiary offices in London, Greenwich, and Austin. We offer two services: personal security for celebrities and executives, and hostage rescue and diplomat security using retired Special Forces soldiers from Russia, Great Britain, and America. We're discreet but gained publicity after freeing sex-trafficked women in Eastern Europe," I said.

"I read about it. That was an impressive achievement," Judd said.

"We're an impressive company. Our directors are retired military and intelligence officials," I said.

Margaret and Randy

Less is sometimes better in marketing so I ended my sales pitch to let Judd's imagination fill in the rest.

My daughter screamed and I cautioned both children before turning back to Judd. He seemed lost in thought, as if deciding how much to reveal. I remained silent, giving him time.

"Did you ever lose anyone?" he asked, finally.

"Lose anyone?" I asked, acting dumb though knowing exactly what he meant.

"Have any of your clients been killed?" he asked earnestly.

This required thinking. Our early clients were threatened businessmen during Russia's Wild West days immediately after the fall of Communism but none had been killed.

"I can honestly say that we've never lost a client. We have good contacts and when danger could be reduced by leaving the country quickly we've been able to arrange it. I've done this several times," I said.

Judd was about to say more when Ada approached.

"We'll talk later," he told me, forcing a nervous smile.

Chapter 24

Later was after dinner while my parents babysat my toddlers. Being a redhead, I instinctively liked redheaded Ada though this made no logical sense. Still, I reassured myself, womanly instincts are often found to be correct after the fact. I greeted Ada warmly.

"How long have you lived in Greenwich?" I asked.

"Not long. You might say that I came with Judd's house, having met him on a charity tour," she replied, with a smile.

His new house was considered an architectural wonder by critics who would sneer at my homey Victorian. But by breaking the neighborhood mold, it wasn't popular. While every Greenwich family possesses the latest gadgets, it is a traditional place. Here, community is what counts and neighbors aren't expected to be surprised which is what Judd's house did. It was unique and, as stated in newspaper descriptions, "for the sophisticated buyer." Meaning, in non-marketing language, that only few would like it.

The house was built of steel embellished with stone, porcelain, tiles, and timber from Europe and Brazil. The ground level was dominated by a thirty-foot high reception hall connected to the second story with a curved staircase. At nearly ten-thousand square feet, it had five bedrooms, five bathrooms, three half-bathrooms, and an immense garage.

Margaret and Randy

Through lofty sliding doors, the main level flowed into a multi-step marble patio with one side of the deck ending in a pool while the other side extended to an outdoor kitchen with a retractable roof. An outdoor shower was tucked into the side of the guest house. Neighbors complained that the house didn't "fit in" and that Judd, a newcomer, wasn't "one of us" whatever that meant. Being one of the few single mothers in town, many probably said that about me, I thought.

"I've heard about the house," I said, neutrally.

"Anything good?" Ada asked, with a smile.

"Greenwich is an old-fashioned town," I said, diplomatically.

Chapter 25

In contrast to Judd, Ada was as bubbly as the proverbial spring chicken had it spoken with an Australian accent.

"You're from Australia," I said.

"Don't hold it against me," she said.

"Never. What brought you here?" I asked.

My curiosity was real. Though having traveled as far east as Tokyo, I had never been to Australia.

"Beside Judd you mean," she said, affectionately slipping her arm inside his.

His lack of response surprised me. What troubled him must be far from small, I decided.

"I do public relations for Qantas and was on their maiden, nineteen-hour flight from Sydney to New York."

"That must have been something. How did you manage to survive it?" I asked.

This reflected more than inquisitiveness. I planned to take my toddlers to visit relatives in Berlin and London and was already concerned. Nineteen-hours was far longer than our travel time.

Margaret and Randy

"It beat having to survive the hell-hole of the Los Angeles Airport," Ada began. "Though an assignment, I love long flights. Relaxing in business class without work and with access to dozens of movies and TV shows. What really bothered me was nasal congestion: I'd taken an allergy tablet and Sudafed before takeoff and my head felt like a beehive.

"While lounging in pajamas with kangaroo figures on the front, like we'd been inducted into an adult slumber party, I watched a show about a hit man who joined a Los Angeles acting group. Others drank wine to help them sleep or did calisthenics in back of the plane.

"The food began with tomato soup and was followed by sea bass and dark chocolate and tea. Hours later came potato soup and sandwiches. Everyone lay down when the lights went out. Some fell asleep on the spot but I took an Ambien. Upon awakening, the crew, who'd slept in shifts, looked fresh but the passengers looked bedraggled. Breakfast was an omelet with potatoes, kale, and spinach."

"How did you feel upon landing?" I asked.

"What you might expect. Judd picked me up and I dozed until reaching Greenwich. I was better after walking in the sun a few minutes."

"Thanks for the information. It'll help in the future," I said.

"I heard about you. Maybe you can help Judd," Ada said, gripping my hand.

Chapter 26

Because of its wealth, Greenwich is a privacy conscious town and Ada's comment caught me off guard. Which of my secrets did she know? I wondered, giving her a quizzical look.

"Oh, nothing bad. Just that you've helped others," she said, with a smile.

"We try to. What's your problem?" I asked Judd.

He had been wringing his hands, which is an unusual behavior for an experienced lawyer. By early in their legal career they'd heard just about everything. But those crises aren't personal, I reminded myself.

Finally, as if having decided, his hands ceased moving and he opened up.

"I have two worries. Both are devastating and one could be fatal," he said.

I nodded to indicate that I was listening and awaited more.

"One is financial. That you can't help me with," he said.

When he remained silent, I asked an encouraging question.

"Lawyers earn good money and my father considers you exceptional. Your services must be in demand. Does your financial problem involve gambling or drugs?" I asked, trying to keep disdain from my voice.

These issues can be impossible to resolve as our experiences with several celebrities had taught us. Settle them and *then* call us, we thereafter instructed.

"If it were only those," Judd said, with the barest smile.

Again, I waited.

"I made a big mistake when I stopped working with your dad but was greedy. I considered him old-fashioned and wanted the bigger bucks and greater prestige that an international law firm could provide. So I jumped ship into Manhattan and my blunder. A nightmare can't begin to describe it," he said, as Ada reached for his hand.

"The money was less than you were led to believe?" I asked.

"No, it was what they promised but I didn't understand what came with it, the compromise I had to make," Judd said.

Margaret and Randy

Chapter 27

As Judd paused speaking, I began thinking why I had sensed an affinity with Ada, despite we both being redheads of course. Those knowing me best said that I seemed happiest when ignoring the sensations of fear and flirting with danger, that I had a wicked sense of humor and could make something out of nothing. Did Ada possess these traits too? I wondered, as Judd resumed speaking.

"Your dad and I were collegial law partners and I assumed that would be my future role in my new job too. In my eighth year there, three hundred of us gathered to toast another banner year. We were the second highest-grossing law firm in the world earning nearly four-billion-dollars with each of us taking home between three and eighteen-million-dollars," he said.

"That sounds great to me," I interjected, before scolding myself for interrupting.

My lawyer-dad had long before instructed me to *never* interrupt a client's flowing story.

"It would seem so until learning that there would now be *two* classes of partners. One holding no equity in the firm and earning no more than one-million, one-hundred-thousand-dollars a year. Which is a comfortable living except for the second-class status associated with it. Hardly what one expects after joining a venerated partnership.

Margaret and Randy

"The traditional law firm model and culture are dead. Today, law firms are partnerships only in name. Full-time CEOs, some without a law degree, have replaced the senior partner who formerly oversaw the human resources and accounting departments. Even law firm names are shorter and snappier.

"Law firms have gotten huge. How can you be real partners with those that you don't know?" asked Ada.

"You can't!" Judd replied, angrily. "Now, lawyers are considered expendable and partners will jump to a competitor for the right amount of money, taking their clients as they leave. Junior lawyers have always worked painfully long hours before promotion to partner which meant lifetime tenure. Today, making partner can take over ten years and even then requires scraping for new business. I can't stand working there but also can't afford to leave, not with the cost of my mortgage and divorce settlement. Being a partner is like winning a pie-eating contest where the prize is more pie."

Judd's grim expression kept me from smiling.

"Tell her your *big* problem," Ada said, supportively.

I waited.

Chapter 28

"You heard about the Billionaire Row murders two days ago," Judd said, implying that I must have.

"No," I said.

Judd looked at me with surprise, as if I were a unicorn standing on its head.

"My child was sick. I've been out-of-touch," I explained.

He accepted my ready excuse. Though false, it was better than saying that I'd been too depressed to care about the larger world.

"Billionaire Row is a swath of land around Manhattan's Fifth-Seventh Street where billionaire's vie for the newest, most elaborate apartment. One couple has two with each costing over fifty-million-dollars. Another's cost two-hundred-thirty-eight-million-dollars," Judd said.

"It's their money. Whatever makes you happy," I said, though considering such purchases foolish.

"I agree," Judd said, picking up on my attitude. "But for one family who lived there it no longer matters. They were horribly tortured and murdered. Everyone was killed, including their two poodles. The man's fingers were cut off, joint by joint, his ears were cut off, his eyes were gouged out, and he was castrated. They probably left his tongue so he could speak. His wife and fourteen-year-old daughter were raped and more. Their toddler son was only shot. The castration detail wasn't publicized. A senior partner got the police report," Judd said.

"How are you involved?" I asked.

"He was a co-worker at my firm. We handled some complex international tax work together."

I waited. Judd hadn't fully answered my question.

"A message was on the wall, in the room where his body was found. Written in blood using his finger as a marker."

The silence grew longer. Ada continued holding Judd's hand supportively.

"The words on the wall read, 'Give it or we will return,'" he said, finally.

"Give it or we will return," I repeated.

"*That's* why Judd needs your help," Ada said.

Chapter 29

I understood why Judd worried. I would worry too.

"What do they police say?" I asked.

"They're investigating."

"That's it?"

"That's it."

"They made no offer of police protection?" I asked.

"They said it's not their job, that private security is a task for private companies. *Unless* I have information qualifying me for the Witness Protection Program."

"Do you?" I asked.

"Not that I'm aware. The project we worked on seemed legitimate to me," Judd said.

"What do you want?" I asked, after more silence.

"Safety."

"Okay, to sum up the situation. Your co-worker and their family were murdered. That torture was involved indicates that the murderers were seeking information which they apparently didn't get. Having failed, they leave a message stating they're still looking. You don't know who they are or what information they want. Is this accurate?" I asked.

Margaret and Randy

"Yes. Ada's involvement with me endangers her too," Judd said.

"Personal security is expensive. A minimum of two-thousand-dollars a day for an indefinite period until the murderers are caught. Would your firm cover the cost?" I asked.

"I doubt it. We do international travel and they don't provide kidnap insurance which is pretty standard. Anyway, I plan to quit and my house is up for sale. What value is one's life?" Judd asked.

What value indeed? I thought.

"How soon can you provide it?" Ada asked.

"Our Texas office could supply agents quickly. Until they arrive, you can stay with me. They'd likely want security changes made to your home anyway."

"Is your house safe? Would our presence place your family in danger?" Ada asked.

"My home is as well-protected as the White House," I said, assuredly.

What else could I say though intending to park my children with Erika. Her home, lived in by a billionaire's family, *is* as secure as the White House.

Chapter 30

My final instruction to Judd and Ada, before they left to pack for their stay with me, was for him to think about the projects that he'd worked on, whether any seemed sketchy, not illegal but not fully legal either. As soon as they left I called Cody, the manager of our Austin office.

I like Cody. Just before retiring as chief of the Texas Rangers, he was interviewed on TV. What he said so well accorded with our company philosophy that I was ordered to hire him at far higher than his government salary. What Cody said was "There is a justice of the courtroom and a justice of God."

He picked up on the third ring.

"Margaret, I just got back from Berlin where they raved about you," he said, exuberantly.

"Only because my father is the boss," I said, modestly.

"No, it was from Hedy, a BND officer (the *Bundesnachrichtendienst*, Germany's Federal Intelligence Service). When will I see your children to tell them that their mama is a Texas sheriff?" Cody asked.

I had once worked with Hedy and, following a successful assignment in Austin, was appointed an auxiliary Deputy Sheriff.

"Soon," I promised, and got down to business.

Margaret and Randy

"We need two bodyguards for an endangered couple. His colleague's entire family was tortured and murdered. No one knows why and he fears he may be next," I said.

"You need human rat snakes," Cody declared.

"What are they?" I asked, having never heard the term.

"Huge constrictors that feed on rodents and birds. They grow to eight-feet long and are mostly skittish but some species are docile and make attractive pets."

"But that's not what you're sending me," I said.

"No. I'm sending you two killers," Cody said.

Chapter 31

My invitation to Judd and Ada reflected more than courtesy. Their safety was now my duty and had we a ready safe house I would have sent them there. Our usual clients were super-rich celebrities requiring bodyguard service to protect them from crowd-crushers, not needing protection from crazed killers.

Their speedy return revealed their anxiety, which it was my job to reduce. Nervous clients who don't follow orders endanger others in addition to themselves.

I showed them to their bedroom and adjoining bathroom which contained the usual hotel amenities. Down the corridor, on each floor, was a steel lined security room containing a porta-potty and independent electric, telephone, and air supply systems.

"If an alarm sounds, indicating that the premises have been breached, lock yourself in the nearest security room until the all-clear," I said.

At their startled looks, I added, "The security rooms haven't yet been needed. We'll find you more permanent quarters when your bodyguards arrive from Texas."

"Are they good?" Judd asked, his anxiety not yet eased.

"They're very experienced," I said, not considering that using Cody's words, "two killers," would sound professional.

Margaret and Randy

Erika arrived without an invite to join us for lunch. Being as close as sisters, giving notice wasn't needed. After vague introductions in which I described Erika as my friend and Judd and Ada as my guests, the conversation was blessedly ordinary.

Erika considers herself a *serious shopper* with her long-favored store being Manhattan's Bergdorf Goodman. Being in her final weeks before delivery, I expected that she would have other concerns but, I reminded myself, shopping is her way of relaxing.

"Have you been to Nordstrom?" Ada asked.

"Not yet," Erika said with a smile, patting her swollen belly.

"It's 57th Street's new marvel. A seven-level store where shoppers can get everything from express tailoring to spa services and even Botox. It has seven upscale restaurants and bars, nineteen-foot ceilings, and specially designed artwork. I was there opening day and the crowds were so thick that shoppers trying on shoes had to take numbers like at a deli counter," Ada said.

As Erika's face shone with a relaxed glow, Judd looked tensely about the room as if expecting an imminent attack. I'd better change the subject, I decided.

Chapter 32

"I've just married, which is admittedly late after having two children but we weren't ready. We both work and still seek the blissful solution for a dual-career couple. Did you come to any helpful conclusions while you were married?" I asked.

My ploy worked for Judd managed a wry smile.

"A few things though they didn't help considering how things ended. Other things can sink a relationship, like getting a lover." Judd said.

I waited silently and he continued.

"What worked is writing our contract."

"Writing a contract?" Ada asked, with surprise.

This was obviously the first that she heard of it.

"Oh, not lawyerly legalese but a sense of what we each wanted in life. Failing to decide these had wrecked our previous relationships and we wanted different. We asked what a meaningful relationship meant for each. What we were willing to give and wanted and the lines that I wasn't ready to cross and you had better not cross. Things like that."

"That's so sensible it's surprising you two divorced," I said, taking mental note of what he had said.

"Yes, but what changed was change. Personal decisions can't be set in concrete. People change and there are new decision points. Life throws surprises and love strains to adjust, causing a need to re-contract at transition points like career changes.

"Work was central to our identities and we had both experienced relationships in which our commitment to the other person felt at odds with our dedication to work. We were kind, supportive partners until becoming resentful and restless. We both believed that love and work are separate domains which need reconciling but loving your work eventually leads to bitter conflict until you learn to work your love too. That didn't happen with us and I've vowed to change with Ada," Judd said.

Ada took his hand and this time their smiles were genuine.

Chapter 33

Our lunch turned into a confessional of long buried feelings.

"As a teenager, only three things scared me: sex, God, and being alone. I conquered the first two but never the third which is why I married the wrong man," Ada said.

Her words overlay the tension in the room and caught our attention. Even Erika, who had nervously patted her belly while Judd spoke, looked captivated.

"It was lucky that we didn't have children. Everyone said divorce hurts but so long as there aren't children it's not an irreparable damage like with a full-blown family, that ours was just the broken dreams of two consenting adults. People congratulated me so often about not having kids that I was tempted to pass out party cookies saying, "It wasn't a girl or a boy.""

That Judd now sprawled casually pleased me. There would be nothing calming about the sober instructions from his bodyguards when they arrived. Meanwhile, Ada continued.

"I genuinely believed that I would feel relieved after the divorce since our marriage was a state of desperation for both of us. So much that there was no dispute about splitting things. But afterward, instead of feeling free, my pain varied

Margaret and Randy

from a severe cramp to a mild ache. My therapist told me this was natural for any kind of split."

"Like when a child wants to split from their family but feels homesick at camp," Erika suggested.

"Are you saying I'm homesick for my ex?" Ada asked, angrily.

"Not at all. But after you split, no matter how bad the relationship was, you feel loss. You were used to your marriage. It was comfortable.."

"But it wasn't."

"I didn't mean it like that but in the sense that it was familiar," Erika corrected herself.

To close this painful subject, Erika invited them to visit her home when it was convenient.

Chapter 34

The following morning, Judd and Ada's two bodyguards were announced by my outer door's video surveillance system. Franklin and Carlos were physically similar, being well over six foot and blond. Despite their pronounced Texas drawl, I soon learned that both spoke Spanish fluently, having Mexican grandparents. Also that they were brothers, having the same mother but different fathers.

"She was a poor, tall Norwegian. Our short fathers descended from wealth and wanted a compliant wife which she wasn't," Franklin said.

"Nor are our wives," Carlos confided.

Judd and Ada stared silently as we spoke and I understood. Their lives now depended on Carlos and Franklin, of whom they knew only that they were congenial. It's time to instill confidence, I told myself, turning toward them.

"I don't know what Cody told you so I'll summarize the situation. Judd's law colleague and his family were brutally murdered, leaving a scene like drug cartels use to terrorize. The wife was raped and her husband was cut to pieces, apparently for information which he refused to give or didn't have. Judd is frightened, particularly since he's clueless why this happened as are the police.

Margaret and Randy

"Judd is selling his house and moving. Your job is to protect them until the mystery is solved and the danger past. I'll provide whatever assistance you need including weapons," I said.

"We brought ours on the private flight," Carlos said.

I nodded understanding. Some fly privately just for such a reason. Franklin turned toward his charges and spoke the cruel words that were needed. Brutality had been done and only force could protect them now.

Chapter 35

"What do you hope for?" Franklin asked.

"To be lucky," Judd said, quickly.

"No, not just that though it's always important. Luck isn't a matter of survival in the world you've entered. You either survive or surrender, which isn't possible with these creatures, not to dignify them as people.

"Luck belongs in the cities like when you're crossing a street and momentarily glance at your phone and are hit by a car. Now, here, it's like life in the wilderness where wolves don't kill unlucky animals but only weak ones. Do you want to be weak or to survive?" Frank asked.

"To survive, of course," Ada answered.

"Then you must do exactly as we say, even when our instructions seems excessive or to not make sense. Have either of you ever killed anyone?" he asked.

"No," Judd answered for both.

"My question was rhetorical, to emphasize the seriousness of our job. We *have* killed, in the military and elsewhere, and these deaths didn't cost us a moment of sleep. The dead were snakes and we're rat snakes, the constrictors that feed on rodents but can be attractive pets too. Do you have any questions?"

Margaret and Randy

"Will you accompany us all the time?" Judd asked.

"Only when you're outside which won't be often. We won't interfere with your personal lives."

"It already feels different," Judd declared.

"That's inevitable. We're requiring you to change and when one finds themselves doing unlike what they usually do, they feel themselves another person, as if they'd been teleported into another life. It takes poise to face reality and overcome fear," Carlos said.

"Life has become dangerous," Judd mused.

"Being alive is dangerous and fatal in the end," Franklin said.

We all smiled. They were slight smiles but smiles nevertheless.

Chapter 36

"The most important safety advice that I can give is to trust your instincts. Humans, like all animals, have a reptilian streak to warn them of danger. Whenever you feel uneasy, act on this feeling because you should!

"Hopefully, you won't experience this when you're with us since it's our job to keep danger away. We try to anticipate it but obviously this must be imperfect. Still, we've never lost a charge, which is which what you two are, and don't expect to," Frank said.

"And now?" Judd asked.

"Now, let's eat," he said, accompanying these calming words with a reassuring smile.

We did.

Mothers know that eating reduces anxiety so I'd set relaxing breakfast food though being unsure when Franklin and Carlos would arrive. I had long known that I lacked cooking skill and confined my efforts to the simple dishes of French Toast and cornbread. These always turned out well and I added my favorite of baked salmon. Anything else I order from a local restaurant or Whole Foods. To accompany the meal with soothing conversion, I changed topic.

"Why did you choose to become a lawyer?" I asked Judd.

Margaret and Randy

My ploy worked and he visibly relaxed.

"Because I hated medical school," he said, with a wry smile.

"Okay, and?" I asked, with a quizzical look.

"Tell them!" Ada insisted playfully, putting down her coffee cup.

So Judd did.

"Kids early-on decide what they'll do though maybe changing their mind ten times before fixing on a vocation. Wanting to be like their father and then... My father was a doctor so I decided to be one, went to medical school for a term and hated it."

"Tell them about your summer jobs at the funeral home and department store and factory," Ada said, smiling.

Chapter 37

"I always wanted independence and, as a teenager, worked summers on office jobs at local businesses. My first was at a funeral home, which wasn't as depressing as you might think. The sight of dead bodies didn't creep me out so maybe I'd have made an okay doctor," Judd said.

"You've become a much better lawyer than you ever would a doctor," Ada said, supportively.

"I think so too," Judd said with a small smile, before continuing.

"On each job I learned a good business lesson. From the funeral home it was to meet and enhance your customer's expectations. Around each body was placed colored lights. When I asked, 'Why,' I was told, 'Why have flowers?'

"The department store job taught me a similar lesson. I had been assigned to the Young Men's section which made sense since I was sixteen. I helped a woman buy her twelve-year-old son's suit for his sister's wedding and she asked me to help her choose his shirt and tie in a different section of the store. My instructions had been to not leave my section but I felt that doing so would be the right thing. I helped her make the purchases and returned to my section where I found my supervisor waiting for me.

"She asked where I'd been and, despite my reasonable explanation, criticized me and said she'd tell Mr. Garrison, the store's owner. She did and he called me to his office. I described what happened and said that by helping the woman I'd satisfied her and might have made her a lifelong customer which was what I believed was wanted. Instead of firing me, Mr. Garrison smiled, said that I'd behaved correctly, and handed me a hundred-dollar bill as bonus.

"At the electronics factory I worked as an all-around gofer. The phone rang while I was in the office and I answered it because no one else was around. It was the boss' wife and she wanted to tell him that she'd be late coming home from a club meeting. I promised to do so and when his secretary returned, I told her about the call.

"I'd never liked this woman and felt that she didn't like me. Looking slyly, she told me that the boss was in the executive gym and to give him the message. I went there and was confronted at the door by a naked woman who asked what I wanted. I told her that I had a message for the boss, just as he walked over dressed in a large towel. I gave him the message and returned to the office. 'Did you give him the message?' the secretary asked. 'Yes,' I said. When the boss returned to the office, he told me to never go to the gym again.

"Judd learned to satisfy needs," Ada said, accompanying her double-entendre with a smile.

Margaret and Randy

Chapter 38

As a mother, having business clients as live-in guests was never my choice. When my toddlers were younger, several had stayed in my home briefly and it worked out being convenient, saving me having to manage another setting, and helping me to know the clients better.

While most were likable, none had been so enjoyable as Judd. Fascinating stories erupted from him either from tension or our being an appreciative audience. That his bodyguards enjoyed them showed they were on the same wavelength which would make all safer.

Three days passed during which we awaited new information about the slain family or Judd and Ada's plan for their next move. Guilt from having abandoned my mothering duties caused me to bring my children home just before the news of more murders surfaced. Afghanistan is less dangerous than Judd's firm, I thought, before sharing this information.

Judd and Ada were watching the BBC version of *House of Cards*, which is nastily better than its American version, when I interrupted.

"There's been a development. How well did you know Jackson Leach?" I asked Judd.

"Not well, just for a few months. The lawyer on an anti-trust case came down with mono and I was drafted to take his place. Why? What's happened?"

Margaret and Randy

There was no way to sugar-coat the event to reduce its terror but I tried.

"It may not be related but the bodies of he and his girl-friend were just found in her apartment," I said.

Chapter 39

Judd and Ada accepted my shocking news calmly. They already found themselves doing unlike what they usually did and had gained the poise that comes from facing reality and overcoming fear.

"Were they murdered like the others?" Judd asked.

"There was little difference," I said briefly.

Sharing the details would only create greater anxiety.

"It must relate to a project that you both worked on. What was it?" I asked.

Though being hired to protect, not investigate, the more that we knew about the situation the better service we could provide. Investigating is a police job, not ours. Still, not doing so can arouse disaster, as happened when the Japanese attacked Pearl Harbor in nineteen-forty-one and New York City and Washington were attacked sixty-years later. Catastrophes are rare in the business world but the risk never vanishes.

Judd's expression suddenly changed as if he had a hunch. A solid hunch means that you've fit together pieces of a puzzle quicker than you can think. At that moment, perhaps because of what was said or a random thought, things fit together.

"Do you know what the Egmont Group is?" he asked.

Margaret and Randy

"No," I said.

"It's a network of one-hundred-sixty national financial intelligence units providing a secure internet system through which members share information about money laundering, tax fraud, and other financial crimes.

"Members can exchange information but only through channels which safeguard security equal to that of the Egmont Secure Web. Jackson and I were checking out rumors of problems."

Chapter 40

"What kind of problems?" I asked.

"Serious enough to get the Vatican Bank suspended from using Egmont information," Judd said.

"That must have been a blow to its financial credibility, and the Pope too," I said.

"It was and raised concern among many police agencies. Imagine what might be done since Egmont's function is to prevent financial crimes. It would be like telling burglars which high-end stores lack alarms and giving them police schedules."

"Leaving bank doors open at night," I mused aloud.

"Yes."

"What were yours and Jackson's tasks during this probe?" I asked.

"Correlating who had access to Egmont's log-in credentials with when these were used and the files that were opened."

"These facts wouldn't be useful to a criminal. What information would be worth so many lives?" I asked.

"Egmont's master passwords," Judd said.

I looked at him quizzically.

Margaret and Randy

"The credentials which allowed one to smash the system," he said.

"They *would be* valuable," I said.

"Immensely. Web pirates could then plunder freely. Only synchronized international policing is what keeps them at bay, inadequate though it is," Judd said.

None could argue with that, there being regular reports of intrusions into corporate websites and painful thefts from individuals.

"Did you or Jackson know the master passwords?" I asked.

"No, but we knew how to get them."

"Which is the same as having them," I said.

Judd didn't bother responding to my rhetorical statement. Instead he asked, "What now?"

"Have you told the authorities what you've told me?" I asked.

"No, I didn't realize it until now."

"Perhaps they should be told," I said, tentatively.

My hesitancy didn't derive from doubting what would be best but because this decision must be his. He hired us to manage his security, not to make his crucial life decisions. He's not a child and I'm not his mother, I told myself. *But I am a mother*, I reminded myself, with no small feeling of guilt.

Margaret and Randy

Chapter 41

Having business guests at home didn't require me to shepherd them. We had previously put them up in a local hotel with their bodyguards in a neighboring room. But concern arose from its owner who feared a shoot-out of Hollywood proportion. For the same reason, apartment rentals were out-of-bounds and buying a house for business would run afoul of the town's tight zoning regulations. Thus did these "guests" come to live at my home.

Since this rarely occurred it hadn't yet been a burden. The well-paying clients were congenial and appreciated by our corporate accountant. Moreover, they had been the source of many referrals, much as a skillful doctor is recommended to friends.

I had stopped at a toy store for needed supplies. Four-years of age is when a child moves from their family into the larger world and needs support. As the first grandchildren in the family, James and Donna were spoiled rotten so I had a hard time deciding what to buy, finally settling on the Sorry board game and chapter books to read to them. Hoping that my appearance would be gift enough and not usually being disappointed for they often clung to me upon sight, being unwilling to let go as was I of them.

"How are your houseguests doing?" my father asked during a visit.

Margaret and Randy

"Settling in and deciding on their next move. Have you heard anything?" I asked.

Being a judge, he was clued into the latest crime news.

"No more murders than the latest two, you mean. Thankfully not," he said.

And with this, we focused on the children.

Chapter 42

Children squabble when they want adult attention. So, believing that instilling a love of reading is a crucial parenting task, I turned to reading to them from one of the books that I brought.

Kids' daydream about dogs: wanting one and scheming against parental resistance to get it, which is formidable in my family. Invariably, mothers become the caretaker of a family's animals no matter what others had vowed. Not intending to add this task to my duties, I hoped that reading about four-legged creatures would be enough.

The book contained humorous ink and watercolor pictures about a poodle and a dachshund and a boy and a lonely man. It earned such enjoyment that I also read the other book I bought which told how a grandmother became convinced that their tiny apartment was large enough for a dog. As I closed the book, their grandmother turned toward my children and asked, "How would you like a dog?"

Joy filled their faces as I threw her as dirty a look as one can give their mother. Into this awkward moment, my father motioned me over for his parenting talk.

"There are similarities between raising children and being a boss," he said.

As the holder of both roles, I perked up."

Margaret and Randy

"Leadership is about nurturing your team, creating strong relationships of trust and connection. It shouldn't require a special occasion to build connections at work any more than you wait for a special occasion to connect with your children.

"So before a group meeting or a one-on-one conversation, begin with brief conversation unrelated to the business at hand, making eye contact and smiling before getting down to work. Building this into every interaction will speed your path toward effective collaboration and avoid the pitfalls of misunderstanding and mistrust."

"Okay," I said, to indicate that I was listening closely.

"Recognize that *your* emotional issues can be triggered by others, whether employees or children, and think about the unresolved issues instead of simply snapping. If they're overly dependent, work with them by gradually removing your support. As is done with a child who fears going to sleep, remaining with them until they do and gradually putting them to bed with less cuddling as they learn to put themselves to sleep."

"So I must recognize the hidden stresses they may be dealing with," I said.

"Right! They may want tagless shirts just as you don't want to sit in an uncomfortable chair. It can take a bit of detective work to discover the stressors," my dad said.

"Just now it's not really about a dog but the job crises I must resolve," I said.

Margaret and Randy

"It can sometimes take a newcomer to create order where insiders see only chaos. You'll work them out," he said, confidently.

Margaret and Randy

Chapter 43

Even grownups sometimes need a parent and I had needed one then. What my father said made good sense: that my life felt chaotic and I must impose order on it.

I began by itemizing my current responsibilities: the continuing needs of my toddlers, James and Donna, and my husband, Randy; keeping Asya and Judd and Ada safe as their futures were being decided; and removing the blackmailer from Erika's life. These tasks seemed more manageable once I listed them.

I arranged them by order of urgency with Judd and Ada being first. Their safety had already been dealt with since they were now surrounded by experienced bodyguards. Nor was Asya unsafe since she lived in the same house and enjoyed similar protection. Mila, my personal bodyguard, also lived in my home, which contained security rooms and defensive weapons. Thus my immediate task seemed to free Erika from her blackmailer.

An extortionist is a criminal who is willing to create untold misery for personal gain. Betraying Erika's trust made her murderous feeling toward him understandable. Eliminating her fear required destroying the embarrassing sex videos. And punishing the criminal too? Perhaps, though the healing effect of revenge is over-rated, I thought.

Personal matters continually intruded even as I planned. Within any several days I might experience joy at my

Margaret and Randy

husband's business accomplishment, my child's illness, or having to cope with an imminent danger toward another client.

Was it sensible to choose my lifestyle of continuing multiple demands? Wouldn't my life be easier as a stay-at-home mother, one that our finances could well afford? Absolutely! So why didn't I? I asked myself.

Probably for the same reason that a Good Samaritan jumps into a raging river to save an animal. Though not being logical, their behavior makes sense on another level. Logic doesn't explain everything and a wholly rational view of behavior leads to superficial judgment. Simply put, I was doing everything that I was doing because I felt that I must. Which was a good enough reason for me.

Chapter 44

My decision to help Erika first also had personal roots. I knew how difficult the final weeks of pregnancy are and that anything done to reduce a woman's stress is a blessing

Though Erika didn't know where Clive was, his past friends and family might. Interviewing them must come first, I decided, as later scenarios ran through my mind. Planting drugs and alerting the police could land him in jail and away from Erika but not insure that the sex tape wouldn't become public. Trapping him legally in blackmail would involve the same risk.

The more that I considered involving the authorities the less I liked it. I had promised Erika to *permanently* relieve her worry, not have her settle for a maybe. She was as close as my sister. There must be no *maybe*.

Further thinking produced a solution, which I decided to confirm with someone who was more experienced and ruthless. Mila, my family's bodyguard, was such a person and we spoke as my children played.

Mila had been a police officer in Russia, a medical doctor, and an officer in Russia's Special Forces. She had known hard cases and persons. I described Erika's dilemma.

"The original and all copies of the videos must be destroyed and Clive's disturbance in her life be permanently ended," I declared.

Margaret and Randy

Mila's advice came quickly.

"You need a frightener," she said.

That had been my conclusion too as I spoke the company motto.

"There is the justice of the lawyers and the courtroom, and the justice of The Prophets and of God."

"Do you have such an employee?" Mila asked.

"No, but I know how to get them," I said.

Chapter 45

Erika's first met her step-sister, Jenna, after her rescue from a European sex-trafficking gang. This was aided by information gained from a local doctor following my suggestion that every sex business needed a doctor to treat sexually transmitted diseases.

Facts about the women's captors was gained by a soldier who, after cutting off one of the doctor's fingers, threatened to remove all of them before beginning on his other appendages. The doctor quickly gave in and, in a generous gesture, was paid for his cooperation. I never learned who this soldier was but knew that I needed him. Only terror, or more, could remove the threat to Erika's life.

My uncle, Borya, is a powerful official in the SVR, Russia's Intelligence Service. Though beloved by my children for his jolliness and elaborate gifts, his nickname of Lucifer (The Devil) suggests another nature.

While in Moscow I had been given two phone numbers to reach him: one went through his Chief Assistant and the other would raise him from the dead or so he claimed. By using the first, I reached him quickly enough.

"Uncle, I need your help," I said.

"Of course," he said.

"It's a private matter, to help a friend who is being blackmailed. I would like to hire the soldier who interviewed the doctor during the sex-trafficking rescue. He will be paid three-thousand-dollars a day plus transportation and expenses. It shouldn't take more than a week and he will return home immediately," I said.

"That's very generous," Borya said.

"The victim is like my sister," I said, simply.

"Family is important to Russians. Artem will arrive in two days. I'll send his brother, Mikhail, too. They're a team," Borya said.

"Thank you!" I said, choking down a relieved sob as my feeling of confidence returned.

Chapter 46

The cliché that a mother's work is never done was particularly true for me since my career was only part of it. And, I often thought, the easiest to deal with. Compared with my occasionally troublesome but normal children and my abnormally non-communicative spouse, the rest was easy. But James and Donna and Randy are just being their usual selves and you'll deal with it, I assured myself.

While the children needed only cuddling, feeding, or the promise of a new toy to settle down, Randy presented a bigger challenge. Even after ten years together, there still seemed much I didn't know of what was going on inside his head. My search for this had brought us closer but the more we talked, the more a significant gap persisted.

During marriage, all wonder who their spouse is when not their usual self. This causes some to eavesdrop on phone calls or secretly rummage through dresser drawers, deciding how much to dig and let lie.

My current angst concerned his business trips. Randy was an attractive man and would always meet fascinating women willing to play. After his uptight adolescence, which contained a one-night affair while tipsy, would he now succumb to sweet talk, give rein to the freer sexuality unleashed by our marital bed?

I worried, called the hotels where he stayed and checked his phone bills and credit card statements. Which I could access since these were corporate accounts and I was a business partner.

Did I have him followed by a private investigator? No, for even jealous me recognized what would be excess. Finally, having found nothing incriminating in the accounts or lipstick smears or forgotten panties in a jacket pocket, I gave up. Deciding that my suspicions reflected just personal insecurity. They do, don't they? I half-assured myself.

Chapter 47

Two days later, Artem and Mikhail checked into the Delamar, a luxurious hotel on the Greenwich Harbor. Our guests loved it for its fitness center, wine and cheese receptions, and weekend harbor cruises.

When informed of their arrival, I advised that they nap for several hours to cope with jet-lag before we met for dinner. My mothering orientation carries over into being a boss, I thought.

Dinner was in the hotel's notable restaurant. Its appetizers of caviar and buckwheat blinis made them feel at home. I chose the vegan salad of squash, navy beans, eggplant, spinach, and tomato. As main dish I ordered smoked salmon (my favorite) which they followed. After this arrived and the waiter departed, I described their mission.

"A wealthy woman is being blackmailed with a sex video that was secretly taken during her relationship with the blackmailer. He'll allegedly hand over the film for a substantial payment but we all know this won't happen since she's an ongoing gold mine," I said.

"Why doesn't she contact the police?" Artem asked.

"Her family is prominent. Publicity would affect their business and her fiancée. She's also in the last weeks of pregnancy and doesn't need more stress. She's a friend and we're as close as sisters," I said.

Margaret and Randy

"You can't pay off a blackmailer," Mikhail declared.

"No, it never works," I agreed. "After locating the blackmailer, your task will be to convince him of the error of his ways and recover the video and all copies. You'll then return home immediately with a substantial bonus. Borya has faith in your abilities."

"He is your uncle?" Artem asked.

"Yes."

"He is a great man."

"Yes," I agreed.

"And if this blackmailer cannot be convinced?" Artem asked.

"Then justice must be rendered," I said.

We understood each other perfectly.

Chapter 48

While Artem and Mikhail relaxed, our investigators searched for information about the blackmailer. This wasn't hard since he left a broad trail. The background that Clive had shared with Erika was largely true.

After Child Protective Services removed him from his drug-addicted parents, he had the good fortune to be adopted by a wealthy couple who gifted him with the best private school education. Being smart, all went well until he fell prey to the drug abuse which devastated his biological parents. After seven unsuccessful treatment programs, his thieving and threats caused banishment from the family and Clive turned to crime.

"We'll find him," our investigator assured me.

I waited anxiously, while encouraging Erika to relax before entering labor. As days passed without development, I tried to reduce *my* worry through repeated phone calls to my mother as she babysat my children at Erika's home.

"They're having a ball but missing you terribly. How are *you* doing?" my mother asked, sensing my distress.

"Better now that I'm talking to you. We should speak more often. I was hoping to wind up something at work and it seems not to be happening. I'm leaning on the wall and feel like it's holding me up," I blabbered.

Margaret and Randy

"You are in a bad way. Why not come over?" my mother said.

"I'm trying to accept that the reality I face isn't what I want," I moaned.

"So are you coming?" my mother persisted.

Wanting to go but also not to leave my home-office lest something break, I hesitated and tried to think of a lighthearted response. When confronting disaster, joking is sometimes the only thing to do but none entered my mind.

"I'll be right over," I said submissively, and instantly felt better.

Margaret and Randy

Chapter 49

The talk with my mother, which Erika and her step-mother, Sara, and her step-sisters, Jenna and Venla, soon joined, turned out to be exactly what I needed. During the previous weeks I had felt I was going crazy, becoming like one of those New Jersey Real Housewives of the TV series. After arriving in America, Jenna had watched it obsessively, saying that she was trying to lose her Finnish accent but we wondered at this explanation. After being rescued from sex-traffickers, she had been treated at our local mental hospital where I began fearing that I was heading.

I understood some of this feeling, having suffered it in the past. Stress from over-work compounded by little sleep and actual danger can cause it, and I knew the remedy before my mother asserted it.

"You're trying to do too much. Caring for a family is one whole job and you have even more when counting what you do for your clients and friends. You must slow down and *think*, which is sometimes the most productive action," she said.

I listened but found my mother's advice hard to accept.

"Life is a war in which evil is strong and goodness can be weak," I said.

"You're not the only warrior," my mother objected.

Jenna entered the conversation on this note.

Margaret and Randy

"At times, when feeling that I would never be free, I'd think of an old American movie I once saw, *White Christmas*. It presents an alternate, idealized world without a dark side. A space where war is forgotten and love and relationships triumph. Doing this let me go beyond my prison, made me feel that I was still part of a community that cared for me and would rescue me as it did," Jenna said, and began sobbing.

Despite being repeatedly raped and beaten, having faith brought her through. Can I do less? I thought.

"You're smiling," my mother observed.

"Yes, I had an idea. Though it's not Christmas, let's watch *A Christmas Story* after lunch. It tells how, after a family overcame calamities, presents are unwrapped and they gather for their meal with the narrator saying, 'All's right with the world.'"

"I loved watching that movie. It gave me the strength to work through hard situations," Erika exclaimed.

And that's what we did.

Margaret and Randy

Chapter 50

As the movie ended, I thought of something I once read which seemed to explain why I had felt so disheartened. That depression is often felt as a gap, a loss of certainty leaving us feeling empty. A chaotic time between the breakup of one's old identity and the creation of the new.

For me it arose because I hadn't fully accepted my dual life as mother and career-woman, resenting each for keeping me from the other. But upon accepting that my nature required both, the hopelessness vanished since only by doing both could I be the mother that my children deserved.

If I dreamed and dared, so too would James and Donna which is the greatest gift that parents can give their children. But pray helps too, asking God for the strength to remain calm despite feeling helpless. Hope for a miracle is always with us, like the rainbow after a storm.

My newfound calm affected the others. Moods lifted and the next hour was spent sharing casual matters: tips on the latest gadgets, local gossip and the like.

"Well, you're in a better mood," my mother remarked as I stood to leave.

"Sometimes even grownups need their mother," I said.

It isn't the first time I said this and won't be the last, I thought.

Margaret and Randy

Mikhail approached as soon as I entered my home.

"Finding Clive was easy but getting to him won't be," he said.

"Why not?" I asked.

"How much do you know about Los Ántrax?"

"Nothing."

"It's an enforcer gang of the Sinaloa Cartel, responsible for many homicides and violent attacks. They provide armed security for drug gangs."

"So?" I asked.

"They've exported their services to the United States. Clive is living in one of their houses," Mikhail said.

Chapter 51

Poise comes from facing reality and overcoming fear and that's what I tried to do. This, even as thoughts of cartel atrocities flooded my mind: the Drug Enforcement Administration agent who was skinned alive with his skin being mailed to his boss; party-goers being machine-gunned during their night out, and more. Cartel members weren't to be trifled with. But was Clive really their partner? Did they permit non-Hispanic members?

"What do you want us to do?" Mikhail asked.

As their boss, it was my decision to make but I wasn't sure. Warring against a cartel was a government's task but solving Erika's problem couldn't wait. I hesitated.

"We'll wait before contacting him. Track his movements to see when he's alone," I said.

Gaining facts and slowly considering them is sometimes the most productive activity, my lawyer-father once told me.

"Will do," Mikhail said, as Victoria and Asya approached.

"Show Margaret what you've learned," Victoria said, proudly.

Margaret and Randy

Asya opened *Little Women*, a coming-of-age novel about four sisters after the American Civil War, and read a page.

"That's *wonderful*! Soon you'll be speaking *perfect* English, " I said, with the exaggerated affect that children appreciate.

Asya's smile indicated that my comment hit home. It was her first smile since we met, on the day of her parents' murder. She went to her room to read.

"She's an unusual child, recovering so quickly, and smart too," I said.

"I want to show you something," Victoria said, reaching into her large handbag.

It was a copy of the photo of a dark-haired child dressed in a light-colored, old-fashioned gown. I looked at it quizzically until it hit me. A solid hunch means that you've fitted pieces of a puzzle together.

"It looks like Asya," I said.

"Yes, doesn't it," Victoria said.

Chapter 52

Talking about Asya led my mind onto other tracks. An inevitable consequence of giving birth is the development of a *mommy-brain,* and marriage brings more according to my longer-married friends. Insight into common male traits like beginning a project and not finishing it and leaving messes for others to clean up and not even understanding what constitutes a mess.

These even feel acceptable if a woman is playing the caretaking role as I was with Asya. Meaning that I did the mothering and her cleaning up,

Because mothers put others first, they have less time to deal with *their* issues. It's as if they volunteered to be second-class citizens who no one thanks for doing the hard stuff. The profits from Mother's Day greeting cards should be given to mothers, I thought.

"Are you listening?" Victoria asked.

"I'm sorry. I was thinking about my kids," I said, giving the forever acceptable excuse.

"The photo," Victoria said.

"Yes," I said firmly, to indicate that I was now listening closely.

"I must tell you some history. Anastasia was the younger sister of the Grand Duchesses Olga, Tatiana, and

Maria, and the elder sister of Alexei Nikolayevich. She was the youngest daughter of Tsar Nicholas II, the last sovereign of Imperial Russia, and his wife Tsarina Alexandra Feodorovna. Anastasia's entire family was murdered by Bolsheviks in 1918."

Victoria continued after pausing for breath.

"But rumor existed of her possible escape, fueled by the fact that the location of her burial was unknown during the decades of Communist rule. Her exact title was Grand Princess."

"She must have had a luxurious upbringing," I said.

"To the contrary. The Tsar's children were raised simply. Sleeping on hard camp cots without pillows except when they were ill, taking cold baths in the morning, expected to tidy their rooms, and to do needlework to sell at charity events when they weren't otherwise occupied."

"So?" I asked.

"I can't help thinking that Asya is Anastasia's biological descendant," Victoria said, with a steady look to emphasize her seriousness.

Chapter 53

"Are you saying that Asya is descended from royalty? That means nothing nowadays," I asserted.

"It could be crucial for some nations. A royal lineage has cachet and not only for selling perfume. It can create stability for a nation like Russia that has had little," she said pointedly.

"But she's a child. No nation would appoint her as ruler," I objected.

"Not now but someday. Having a restored monarchy could be important for Russia which lacks a democratic tradition and can easily descend into tribalism and anarchy. Afghanistan had some measure of calm before its monarchy was overthrown. The United Kingdom's existence is unimaginable without its monarch though the Queen has no real power," Victoria said.

"Russia," I mused aloud.

"There were recent rumors of a failed coup," Victoria said.

"Yes," I readily agreed.

I knew all about it though the details were never made public. Boris, a billionaire oligarch, had plotted the assassination of an American official which was then to be blamed on Russia's president. He would be arrested, Boris become a Stalin-like dictator, and decades of horror be ushered in for a nation that already endured so much.

"The couple that Asya lived with weren't her biological relatives," I said.

"Not likely. The identity of her forebears must have been hidden for generations."

"Until some group discovered it," I said.

"Or groups. Those wanting a Russian monarchy restored and others yearning to revive a dictatorship," Victoria said.

"Russia's president might favor the former. He's encouraged the nation's traditions as by re-establishing the Russian Orthodox Church," I said.

"The murder of Asya's foster parents could be the opening salvo in that war. I can think of no other reason for their killing," Victoria said.

"It would be safest if Asya didn't leave the house," I said.

Victoria didn't argue.

Margaret and Randy

Chapter 54

Victoria's theory about why Asya's foster parents were murdered was the only one that made sense since nothing had been robbed and the victims had no enemies, having lived the customary sedate life of a diplomat family. Their deaths had no political consequence whereas Asya's life could have world-shattering effects if Victoria was correct.

Randy would be home tonight and I would run this hypothesis by his organized mind. *If* he'd listen after learning of our other guests. He hadn't objected to Asya's presence since he loved children and she was demand-free and got along well with our toddlers who considered her an older sister.

But my other guests were a different matter and I expected Randy's protest. Being endangered, Judd's and Ada's presence imperiled our family during their brief stay. Still, had I believed that a serious danger existed I would not have allowed them to remain.

Soon after moving into my house, I converted it into a near fortress with multiple warning alarms, security rooms and weapons, and one bodyguard with more available when needed. Only Erika's home would be considered safer which was why I had sent my toddlers there until things settled.

Yet my talk with Randy would not be easy. Despite our long involvement and having two children together, he had been skittish about marrying though soon becoming hypnotized by its comforting rhythm. But his persistent

Margaret and Randy

longing for the idyllic, television family show atmosphere often conflicted with my career. My mother advised me that couples who talk out issues stay together. The time for writing our marital contract was overdue.

Chapter 55

Because timing is crucial when raising a touchy issue, I waited to speak with Randy. Being relaxed after his favorite dinner would be a good time but sex would unwind him more so I decided for that time. Feeling that I was becoming one of those wives who gave their demanding husband sex to get something even though with Randy it had generally been me who initiated it. Now, lying naked in his arms, I asked how his business trip turned out.

"The past is a dream and the future is a mist. What amuses man is to be puzzled, to not know the outcome of a boxing match or baseball game," Randy said.

"You've become a poet," I said.

"Not me. It's a paraphrase of Muhammad Ali, the greatest boxer, from an old *Sports Illustrated* I found in my hotel room," Randy said.

"Huh."

"But to answer your question: I'm not sure. I tried convincing the DARPA (Defense Advanced Research Projects Agency) people that they needed to stop thinking of programming computers like those that run factories and program them more like babies think," Randy said.

"Babies?" I asked, feeling puzzled.

Margaret and Randy

"Certainly. Understanding how babies think is the key to ensuring AI, artificial intelligence, advancement. Think of it! Human infants are the best learners. Computer algorithms need vast data and aren't good at generalizing from it. Babies learn more powerfully than computers and from messier data. What we must do is create artificial intelligence that does the same.

"AI must now be trained on hundreds of millions of images to pick out the correct ones. The basic principles behind our learning algorithms were discovered forty years ago. We now have massively more data to deal with and massively more computer power but are basically doing the same thing while young children can learn about dogs and lions from a few pictures.

"For a computer to learn, each piece of its data must be selected and the computer given clear rules. In contrast, most baby learning is spontaneous and self-motivated, the parents' role just being to keep them healthy and out of trouble."

I was impressed. Randy is one of the smartest people I know, I told myself, and not for the first time.

"Will DARPA invest in our company?" I asked.

"They're coming around," he said, with a confident smile.

Chapter 56

A comfortable silence followed as we pursued our separate thoughts. His were of business success while mine were whether our work success would extend to our marriage which felt unbalanced. I'll give it my best shot, I decided.

"Randy," I murmured softly.

"Hmm?"

"We must talk," I said.

"Okay," he said, stiffening slightly.

The prospect of talking about personal issues always jarred him.

"We're an ambitious couple and have talked about what we want in our careers but never in our marriage. This scares me," I began.

"What do you mean?" Randy asked.

It's good that he's focusing on what I'm saying, I thought.

"Well, we're been together since Junior High School and have two children but never wrote a contract for our relationship. Not a formal one like lawyers do but simply examining what each of us wants in life, besides having satisfying work of course. It's time."

Margaret and Randy

"That makes sense," Randy said.

I pressed on, believing that I might have been misjudging his ability to connect on emotional issues.

"You have your work projects and I have mine but now the project is us. What each of us is willing to give and wants, the lines that we're not prepared to cross and which we each had better not cross. Issues like that," I said.

"Like we're creating a business plan," Randy said.

"Exactly."

"Who goes first?" he asked.

"Numero Uno. You," I said.

I grinned expectantly, having concluded that our discussion would be easy. But Randy wasn't smiling.

"Who are these terrified strangers in my home and where are my kids?" he asked furiously.

Our home and children have now become "my." This discussion isn't going well, I thought.

I embraced him. This usually calmed him but it didn't now. Yet, expressing his anger was good. Better than having it fester and be expressed in continued nastiness or an affair. And, though I disliked admitting it, his rage at my action was justified. *What had I been thinking?*

Chapter 57

"You're right. I fucked-up," I said.

This admission and use of a crudity which had never before passed my lips, lessened his rage.

"What happened?" he calmly asked.

"Judd is my dad's former law partner and was referred to my company over dinner. He needs protection from an unknown danger. The other men are Judd's bodyguards and Ada is his girlfriend. The FBI and police are involved.

"Arrangements are being made and they'll soon be gone. I should have told you but I expected this before you returned. Meanwhile, the children are staying at Erika's house which is as safe as the White House.

"Renting a house for company clients has been on my agenda for years but I haven't gotten to it and it's not easy to find one in Greenwich. The pre-school that our kids attend is a germ factory and I've had my hands full with doctor appointments though this isn't a good excuse. I apologize for my screw-up and will try not to do it again."

My teary apology aroused his tight embrace. This crisis in our relationship was over but I knew there would be others. It would be inevitable as we aged and our careers changed and our children developed. Sustaining two careers without shortchanging our marriage wouldn't be easy but this is the same dilemma that many modern couples face.

Margaret and Randy

I separated myself from Randy's embrace and reached for the pen and pad on the night table.

"I guess it's time to draw up our contract," I said softly.

"I guess that it is," Randy agreed.

Chapter 58

Neither Randy nor I had bothered dating others after meeting in seventh-grade since our temperaments fit together so well. I was social, he a loner, and we both came from stable, striving families which expected their children to excel, inspiring education and community responsibility from which we both bloomed.

Randy earned a doctorate in computer science from Columbia University and I studied at neighboring Barnard College, dropping out after becoming pregnant during my sophomore year. But the pressures from managing the office of an international security firm and rearing two children hadn't ended my education. I still took classes, though mostly online, and hoped to gain my degree. Probably about when my children graduated from elementary school if nothing interfered.

Our family was financially stable with an (inherited) home. Only emotional challenges remained, which I knew were often the biggest. Thus our contract was a psychological one of sorts.

What came next was more romantic than it sounds. We each wrote answers to the questions that I stated earlier: what scared us, what we wanted, and the red lines that neither of us had better cross. With these in mind. I began.

"We should have done this years ago. Because we didn't, our contract was tacitly set and we often wound up sensing that life was throwing surprises at us with our love straining to adjust. But we're young and it's not too late.

"Work is central to our identities. Yet just as we love our work, we must work our love or angry strains will arise," I said.

"That makes good sense," Randy said.

This *will* work, I thought, smiling as the tension lifted from me.

Margaret and Randy

Chapter 59

When I finished speaking it was as if we had an unspoken agreement that this particular crisis was over though I knew that others were inevitable. Life's transition points would create new stresses to surmount: when future children were born and they eventually left home; as we aged and physically (though hopefully not mentally) declined; the grief we felt when loved ones passed on.

Moreover, our jobs would create new demands. I was being groomed as Chief Executive Officer for the company's main office in Berlin. Would Randy willingly move abroad or this be one of his Red Lines?

"We're combining two parallel lives. What are your Red Lines," I asked Randy.

"I hadn't ever thought that but one is my demand before we married: that you never lie to me, not ever or about anything. Even if you can't always share the confidential work that you're doing," Randy said.

"A vow which I haven't broken," I said.

"My Red Lines are that you remain a great father to our children and never become involved with another woman," I said.

"Those are easy promises," Randy said, with a smile.

Margaret and Randy

I smiled too though my memory of his long past, one-night affair with a fellow college student still hurt. But I raged about it then and reviving the event wouldn't be productive.

"I can imagine two future issues. I'd like the larger family we can afford. How would you feel about that?" I asked.

"Another boy for you and another girl for me," Randy said, with a smile.

More than two, I thought, but didn't say. *That* would be a future discussion.

"Also, our work might demand a move. Mine to Berlin and yours to a high-tech hub like Austin. I know that you don't like change but what about this?" I asked.

Randy's answer was slow in coming but big in surprise.

"I'll adjust to wherever so long as my family is with me," Randy said.

The sex that followed was our best ever. Randy had matured into the man I always hoped for and his words that followed sealed my belief.

"We speak many thousand words a day but those that I think most often are 'I love you.' Whatever I accomplish in life, meeting you will always be the best thing that happened to me."

Randy hadn't stated one Red Line, being sure it wouldn't be crossed: that I never let my work endanger our family.

Chapter 60

Before Randy spoke so passionately, I had obsessed about other wives. Fighting my resentment and jealousy as I pretended to be happy about their good relationship and feeling hurt because it wasn't mine.

This sadness never returned after that night when our relationship became sealed, not in government-based legality but in what felt like the eyes of Heaven. I would have liked to bask in this feeling but earthly matters pressed: Erika's blackmail, Judd and Ada's safety and, most confusing of all, Asya's future.

I focused on Erika's problem first. To reduce her stress before she gave birth seemed crucial lest it harm her unborn baby. I would blame myself if anything happened, irrational though this would be.

Private security agencies do not involve themselves with criminal matters except by providing information to the police. Erika's reluctance to prosecute her former boyfriend, Clive, would remove police interest in the crime. But a Mexican drug cartel operating in the United States was a serious government concern. Still, our interest was with Clive and not the gang. Why would they accept an American as co-worker? What valuable skill did he possess? I wondered.

"What kind of education did Clive have?" I asked Erika.

Margaret and Randy

"Computer security. As a prank, he once hacked into the Federal Reserve Bank's webpage to place a rude message. It got a lot of publicity but he was never caught," Erika said, after a momentary thought.

"*What?*" she asked, noticing my face brighten.

"I just thought how to send Clive to Australia," I said.

"Huh?" Erika asked, having forgotten this juvenile slang.

"Send him down-under for good," I said.

Chapter 61

"My plan requires the sharing of your problem with a lawyer to negotiate an agreement with the government," I said.

"That would take an unusual lawyer," Erika said, hesitantly.

"D. D. Palmer is that. As a teenager he grew marijuana in his father's garden and was arrested for urinating his name into wet concrete. He later wore psychedelic neckties, fluorescent shoelaces, and clothes with lollipop colors," I said.

Erika just stared.

"D. D. has retired locally from being federal prosecutor for the Southern District of New York. He's a friend of my father and has helped me in the past. He's expensive but you couldn't find better," I said.

"What's the plan?" she asked.

"The cartel that Clive is involved with is *hated* by the Drug Enforcement Administration. That's not too strong a word since they skinned one of their agents and mailed the skin to his boss. By using Clive's knowledge, their operations can be destroyed in America and maybe in Mexico too," I said.

"Why would he cooperate and how could that help me?" Erika objected.

Margaret and Randy

"That's why we need D. D. to negotiate an agreement. In exchange for our information, the government will threaten Clive with a death-penalty charge unless he helps them and discloses all his past crimes too. This would include his blackmail of you and turning over the sex video. Its publication would void the agreement and open him to the death penalty. I think he'd be truthful. Your payment was probably small potatoes in his life, his main motive being revenge porn," I said.

"How soon can I meet this lawyer?" Erika asked, after brief thought.

"Immediately," I said, reaching for my phone.

"Margaret, how nice to hear from you. Your father told me how mischievous your toddlers are," D. D. Palmer said, upon picking up my call.

"Like their mother," I said, with a laugh.

"Our families must get together. What can I do for you?" he asked.

I told him.

Chapter 62

"My friend is being blackmailed with a sex video that was secretly made. The man is an American confederate of the Mexican drug cartel that tortured and murdered a DEA agent. She will cooperate in exchange for eliminating the blackmail threat. Were the government to confront the man with a death penalty charge, he might well agree to a plea bargain involving helping the government to destroy the cartel, confessing all his crimes, and surrendering the video and any copies," I said.

"This sounds like the last case you brought me," he said.

"Yes."

Then, a wife provided evidence against her husband's drug gang in exchange for her immunity from prosecution and the government letting her keep the marital assets. It was a good deal, except for the husband and his criminal associates of course.

"Who is your friend?" D. D. asked.

"I know her father," he said, after I told him.

"Erika was in a bad way during her involvement with the man. She's completely changed and will be giving birth in weeks. Anything done to reduce her stress would be a blessing. Her first pregnancy miscarried," I said.

Margaret and Randy

"Come to my house now. Do you remember the address?"

I said that I did and we would be there in ten minutes.

Palmer's house was a large colonial, two miles outside Greenwich. The door was opened by his wife, a tall, casually dressed woman in her fifties who became solicitous upon seeing the very pregnant Erika.

"My husband said you were coming. Can I get you water or anything? D. D. can be forgetful about courtesies," she said.

Erika refused as Mrs. Palmer helped her off with her coat though this wasn't needed. Despite his wife's remark, D. D. did offer us beverages when we entered his home-office, which we refused. Though not wearing the three-piece suit typical of lawyers, his clothes were far from flamboyant with its tan sport-shirt, brown sweater, and pressed trousers. I was hesitant to leave Erika's side though knowing that I must since attorney-client confidentiality exists only when both are alone. As I rose, D. D. said to Erika, "Your father helped me during a rough period. Though barely knowing me, he paid for the surgery that saved my wife's life. I will do all I can for his daughter without fee. Leave your worries with me," he said.

The sound of Erika's sobs accompanied me as I closed the door behind them.

Chapter 63

Mrs. Palmer joined me as I waited in their library.

"Whatever her problem, I've known my husband to perform legal miracles," she said.

"So have I," I said.

A comfortable silence followed with each of us lost in thought.

"Giving birth is tough and harder afterward," she said.

I listened closely, she being a more experienced mother than me. She seemed to have given this advice before and then I remembered that she was a nurse.

"During their early weeks, babies are fussy and colicky but at three months they've gotten their bearings. Adjusted to life outside the womb and forgiven their mother for pushing them from a quiet home into our noisy world.

"By then, mother and baby have negotiated feeding patterns and routines of bathing and play. They're sleeping longer at night and wake up happy in the morning, having traded their newborn frailty for growing toughness. They're also more sociable, eyeing people and smiling at everyone who engages them, even strangers.

"The mother is then closer to full recovery from childbirth, getting more sleep and able to exercise again, weary couples having gained faith that they'll succeed at parenting even as their baby's eyes reflect guileless hope and knowledge of their human potential, of who they'll become."

"You're a wise woman," I said.

"A good marriage gives you that," Mrs. Palmer said, with a smile.

Chapter 64

Erika's relaxed look, upon exiting D. D.'s office, comforted me. Stress during pregnancy can kill and, though I never said it, might have affected her past miscarriage, having read this during my pregnancy. I waited until we left the Palmer home before asking.

"How did it go?"

"He said things that should work out with only my minimal involvement. That he'd start immediately and I should relax," Erika said.

"Did he say what your 'minimal involvement' would be?" I asked.

"To meet Clive in a room observed by federal agents. Once his blackmail proposal was recorded, my job would be over," Erika said.

"You'll need training," I cautioned.

"That'll be arranged and I'm actually looking forward to it. Remember my starring role in the high school musical?" Erika asked.

I wanted to say that there would be no music in this production but simply nodded, expecting her safety to be assured. Many government careers would implode if the pregnant daughter of a billionaire were harmed.

Margaret and Randy

"He gave me good life advice too," Erika said.

"What was it?"

"That bad experiences affect more greatly than good ones so it's important to say 'no' to negativity. That one should relive good moments and see the big picture. I'd become so focused on this problem that I'd been overlooking the good things in my life: being healthy and having a loving family and friends. In the scheme of things, Clive's threat is like the pimples we worried about as teenagers. When's the last time you worried about them?" Erika asked.

I smiled in agreement though stress had caused my face to break out a month before.

Chapter 65

I had been right to worry about Erika's emotional state. As soon as our car pulled away from the Palmer residence, she began speaking of her past miscarriage as if in a trance. I didn't interrupt, sensing that what she needed wasn't kindly words but a caring listener.

"I don't feel this now but I then sensed I would have a miscarriage. My scan, after I had a small bleed, made me feel that maybe it wasn't my baby's time though knowing there is always reason to have hope. And the doctor had been positive, saying that it wasn't bad news. In another week when the baby had grown, I would know if everything was okay.

"My next week was filled with worry but I pretended that everything was alright despite having more bleeding. You were all supportive but nothing anyone said could have helped and everyone knew that. I kept saying to my baby, 'Please don't leave us. You're so loved here.'"

My eyes remained eyes glued to the road as Erika spoke.

"But soon I couldn't deny what was happening, that my baby left us. Clarence's hugs were the most loving moments I ever experienced and the greatest that I ever needed. He held me on the bathroom floor as I howled, having the same feelings but worrying about me.

Margaret and Randy

"The next days were a blur as we hoped for the miracle that somehow our baby had survived. Soon we'll see our safe-and-sound baby on the scan, I fantasied. But I'd already stopped talking about names and bedroom colors. That vanished even before we were told that I was no longer pregnant.

"We stumbled into the waiting room with its boxes of tissues and I thought of all the people who had sat here before. The sunrise mural on the wall might have been to remind people that every day is a new day and life goes on, that they could deal with hurt and loss and nobody has a monopoly on pain. Those who say, 'Now then, you weren't far along,' don't understand. *It was our baby!*"

I waited to cry until Erika entered her home.

Chapter 66

Erika's problem slipped from my mind as other events unfolded. Uppermost was Randy's near ultimatum to get our guests and their bodyguards out of our house. This forced me to find the safe house accommodation for endangered clients which I had long delayed doing. Guilt had resided in the back of my mind so Randy's demand proved a blessing in disguise by ending my dilly-dallying.

I had learned about acquiring commercial space from Erika who accompanied me when I rented the company office in downtown Greenwich. Thanks to her I now felt competent.

The story which I told the realtor wasn't that the dwelling would house endangered clients. No sane owner would have rented it for this. What I said was that I had a large extended family which often visited. That this (fantasied) family disliked staying in hotels and, being elderly and wealthy, their wishes were a must.

Since Greenwich contains many rich eccentrics, my story didn't surprise him. Nor did my requirements that the house have at least five bedrooms and four bathrooms, large acreage, and a gated entrance. Being security conscious, I would pay for upgrades if needed.

After the realtor walked me through four houses, I rented one for three years with a five-year option thereafter at a one-percent increase per year. I learned from Erika that this was considered customary.

Margaret and Randy

This five-bedroom, five bathroom house had been built in 1936 but been impeccably renovated. It was on a three acre lot on Dingletown Road.

Our guests would appreciate its fabulous kitchen and large living room with marble fireplace. The gorgeous master suite containing a deck and spa bath might reduce their worries. But, more importantly, the house vanquished mine since it saved my marriage!

Chapter 67

You might think that with all of Erika's worries she would want to talk about them but instead she wanted to see the house that I'd rented. She had long been an amateur decorator, having re-decorated her teenage bedroom so often that her father threatened to take away her credit card until she asserted that her way of relaxing was better than taking drugs.

Erika approved of the ninety-five-hundred-dollar a month rent that I negotiated which included the appliances but not utilities.

"You can rent furniture too if you promise not to get it bullet-holed," she said whimsically.

"You're in a better mood," I observed.

"But jittery. I'm meeting Clive tomorrow and can't wait for it to be over."

"You'll do fine. I *did* remember your high school play. You got a standing ovation and your dad was afraid you'd want to be an actress," I said, supportively.

"There was no danger of that. I was never that good and knew it. Now, take me around the house," she said.

Erika inspected the rooms with the eye of a realtor and froze when we entered the kitchen.

Margaret and Randy

"Will you look at that?" she said, slowly.

Before us stood an empty glass-door, peek-a-boo refrigerator, the latest appliance and intended to show that its owner loves cooking and entertaining.

"My dad hates ours but I like it. It's the sweet spot where utility meets homey and softens the boring room with color. Still, what *do* people conclude when they see your French's Mustard and Ketchup, and the glass shows every smudge, needing more cleaning than stainless steel," Erika said.

"Or when your child messes its orderliness when getting peanut butter," I said, adding my opinion.

The ring of her phone interrupted our banter and the call changed her mood. When it ended, she turned toward me.

"Clive changed our meeting to later today. I must tell the Feds," Erika said.

Chapter 68

My experiences had taught me that while being insane isn't critical to working undercover it does help. But I didn't share this insight with Erika. Instead, I kept up her spirits by listening as she repeated what her government handler instructed her, fixing it in her mind.

"Haggle about getting the video before handing over the cash. The more threats he makes, the better our video will be, and don't worry since you'll be perfectly safe! We'll shut the operation down if it looks like he'll put a hand on you," she was told.

"What about my having a gun?" Erika had asked.

"No. Acting helpless and naïve is your best protection. Besides, we want him alive and working with us. Though I'd expect that he'd prefer being shot to what the cartel would do to him," the handler said.

"I shouldn't have worried. You'd have been proud of my performance," Erika told me afterward.

"I'm sure that I would," I immediately agreed.

"All went picture-perfect. Whatever Clive's brilliance as a hacker, he's not street-smart. Were I him, I would've set another meeting place to insure against a law enforcement trap. He was grabbed after leaving my room and told his Miranda Rights in the room across the hall. God, but I wanted

Margaret and Randy

to slam him with a baseball bat!" she said vehemently, losing her cool.

"I understand but you must stay calm and save your energy for the delivery room. Let Clive's memory become just a lesson for our kids: to never take off their clothes before a camera," I said.

"The Eleventh Commandment," Erika said.

"Amen to that."

Chapter 69

One problem down, two to go, I thought, the moment that Erika left. After which I went to rent furniture for the safe house. Possessing a woman's judgment and because mostly men would be staying there, I asked my assistant, Jordan, to accompany me.

"I wouldn't be much help. I rely on Elizabeth to furnish our places," he objected, after hearing my request.

"I'm sure your wife does a great job but men see things differently and those staying there will be mostly men under stress. Awkward surroundings can make a difference like putting a military guy in a chintz-decorated bedroom. I want the atmosphere to be home-like, not motel-like. Stylish and elegant but with masculine undertones conveying warmth and strength," I said.

"I'll do my best," Jordan said hesitantly, with the military attitude that *any* order will be achieved.

"That's all I ask," I said, and he did provide good ideas.

"I would think that a masculine room has dark colors with pops of warm metallics like gold or brass to break the color blocks. Clean geometric patterns with sharp edges as opposed to feminine curves and colors, with mixed materials and an absence of clutter," Jordan said.

Following these principles we chose substantial pieces for the library: a sizable oval desk with large ottomans and leather club chairs, and ivory-colored carpeting to balance the walls which would be painted an arresting shade of black.

For the living room we chose a brown leather sofa with pillows and matching chairs, and an upholstered grey sofa with navy pillows. Then added beige and black Moroccan rugs, and a mix of textures emphasizing natural materials of stone and rough-hewn wood. The kitchen was similarly decorated by blending brick and stone with metal finishes. A credenza to hold stoneware and vintage books completed our day's shopping.

"I'd be happy in this house," Jordan said, as we left the furniture rental company's warehouse.

"You had great ideas," I said.

One can't compliment an employee too much.

Chapter 70

After arranging for delivery of the furniture, I shopped for the groceries and amenities that would be found in classy hotels. Housekeeping would be done by my present cleaner, Annette.

I had hired Annette as a full-time corporate employee. Besides cleaning my home and home-office, she provided the minimal cleaning that the company office on the waterfront required. I didn't expect this new task to take much time since residence guests would be few and far between.

Security upgrades on the house would take another week after which Erika and I would inspect its livability, her senses being more critical than mine. Then, Judd, Ada, and their bodyguards would move three miles into their new quarters.

I didn't expect argument about this change but couldn't be sure. Even the smallest shift can upset anxious people though they would be as safe there as in my home. The move would be good for all and I hoped they would view it this way. Yet my nearness had stabilized their daily routine so speaking with them must be my next task, I told myself, hoping for the best.

I feared that our talk wouldn't go well since their only diversion had been my toddlers when they visited their cherished possessions left at home. I had once seen all four engrossed in coloring books. Bodyguards aren't expected to

Margaret and Randy

banter with their charges and so existed on the edge of their days. Interaction with me and my children had granted their lives a semblance of normality. What should I tell Judd and Ada? I asked myself.

One solution would have been for them to remain in my home but this wouldn't have been wise considering Randy's attitude. I entered their bedroom, not knowing what to say but having to say something.

Chapter 71

I told the truth, that my new marriage had hit a rocky point with my husband objecting to strangers living with us. That it had long been my task to find another safe location, one which I hadn't done until now and they would be moving there.

"We understand. We've wondered when he was going to object. Where's the new place," Ada asked, calmly.

"Three miles down the road. It's newly decorated and I'm sure you'll be comfortable. I know staying indoors for a long period can drive one batty so I suggest that you visit my kids occasionally at my friend, Erika's house. Its security rivals that of the White House and the children have grown attached to you," I said.

Ada smiled and Judd nodded silently. My worry had been unnecessary.

Asya had remained when my toddlers were sent to Erika's home. This would have been illogical if there was real danger but the change was done to appease Randy. Asya wasn't our child and James and Donna were. It was that simple.

Not that I neglected Asya. I spent hours teaching her English and engaging in activities that she enjoyed, one being to watch me cook. Which I understood since children enjoy seeing an adult be inept. Toasted cheese sandwiches and

Margaret and Randy

baked apples were the height of my cooking skill, I apparently
having been absent when cooking genes were distributed.

Chapter 72

With her increased English fluency, Asya asked an awkward question, one that reflected an outdated view of families.

"Why were you just now married with James and Donna being so old?"

This was never my intention, I felt like saying but didn't, and tried to think up a simple, honest reply.

"My babies were an accident but loved too. I wanted to marry but Randy wasn't ready. It took him longer to grow up," I said.

Asya nodded and returned to sketching. She had been hanging-out in my home-office each morning, doing her thing while I did mine. It felt comfortable for both of us.

"Judd and Ada left. Will I be leaving too?" she unexpectedly asked, with wide eyes.

Her anxiety was understandable. Would *she* be sent away?

"You're *not* going anywhere! Not until a good home is found for you," I said, emphatically.

"This home is good," she said.

I saw her pain during my slow-to-come reply.

Margaret and Randy

"Asya, we love having you here and haven't thought of you leaving. But the Connecticut Department of Social Services decides where you live. Would you like to stay with us?" I asked.

She silently nodded.

"Alright. My father is a judge and knows politicians. We will invite him for dinner and ask his help. Randy and I would love to have you live with us. James and Donna love you too and you will be their big sister," I said.

While holding Asya as she sobbed, I had several thoughts. My first was that while wanting more children I hadn't expected to adopt one. My second was that I hadn't discussed this decision with Randy and it wasn't one that a person could change if they wanted to live with themselves.

Margaret and Randy

Chapter 73

I spoke with Randy about adopting Asya that night, as a possibility and not my vow since no one likes being ambushed.

"Judd and Ada leaving has made Asya nervous, fearing that she'll be next. Which could be true since, legally speaking, the Social Services Department controls her future. She's delightful and James and Donna love her. It'll hurt them when she leaves. What would you say to our adopting her?" I asked.

"You've always wanted a big family," Randy said.

"Yes."

"She's a wonderful child."

"Yes."

"We can afford the expense of another child."

"Absolutely!"

"An adoption would keep me from fainting during your childbirth," Randy said.

"That's true too," I said, with a grin.

Since childhood, the sight of blood causes Randy to faint.

"Then I'd say it's a go," Randy said.

Margaret and Randy

"It won't be easy. She's a German national and a witness in the investigation of a diplomat's murder," he cautioned.

"You ain't whistling Dixie," I said, using an ancient line.

Having gained Randy's approval, I studied the problem. Like every government-involved issue, what happens depends on who one knows. We needed political allies and I had good contacts thanks to my odd background.

Before conceiving me, my biological mother had simultaneous affairs with two men. Since a DNA test was never performed, my parentage is uncertain and both men consider me their daughter. Which could be awkward except that they like each other, I love them both, and this is what really counts.

One of them, Douglas, is a former British spy living in London. The other, Vladimir, is a retired Russian general living in Berlin. Their security business, which I manage in America, has wide political connections and the Washington friends of my American father could provide more help. It's time to get busy, I told myself.

Chapter 74

Talking about this matter with my father during a family dinner wouldn't work, I decided, since Asya's presence would make our speaking freely impossible. So I made an appointment to see him at his courthouse office.

"This is a welcome surprise," he said, as his secretary closed the door.

"I do love seeing you but also need your help with a problem," I said.

"A legal problem?" he asked.

"Legal and political," I said.

"That sounds interesting and might be more resolvable than a current case," he said.

My dad loves to talk about the law during which he provides paternal guidance about life.

"People usually don't appreciate what they have until it's removed. Like taking sound health for granted until illness comes along or having regular meals until poverty makes this impossible.

"Liberty is also only a term until it's taken away. Then one realizes what it means to have choice and freedom of movement. I again learned to value liberty not by having it taken away but reading a fantastic illustration of its loss. Have you read about the blond-haired killer?" he asked.

"The young man who raped and killed a girl. He was sentenced to death, wasn't he?" I asked.

"Yes, until an energetic lawyer investigated his case and the verdict didn't seem just. For one thing, the eyewitness who identified him turned out to be color-blind and of low IQ. Moreover, at the time of the murder, the defendant had been driving with the girl's father far from the crime. But the case aroused such demand for closure that the detectives viewed it with tunnel vision. They had their man and that was it."

"So was this prisoner released?" I asked.

"No, though to provide time for a new investigation, the governor commuted his death sentence to life imprisonment. But by that time the man believed to be the murderer and crucial witnesses were long gone so an innocent man languishes in jail. Hopefully, your problem will have a happier ending," he said.

"So does my entire family," I said, and told him why I'd come.

Margaret and Randy

Chapter 75

"We want to adopt Asya," I began.

My father leaned closer to show that he was listening carefully.

"Which will be difficult since besides being an apparent German national, she's a witness to a diplomat's murder and under the supervision of the state's Social Services Department. Asya doesn't want to leave us and Randy and I and the children have grown to love her. I don't know where to start or if her adoption is even possible. What do you think?" I asked.

"It may not be as hard as you think. Having been witness to a murder, her life could be imperiled and if she has no biological relatives, American courts are required to consider the best interests of the child. Which one would think would be to remain with you," my dad said.

"Where do I start?" I asked.

"With a good lawyer. How has D. D. helped your other clients?"

"Wonderfully," I said.

"After consulting him, raise the problem with your Berlin contacts while he does the same in Washington. If necessary, our congresswoman might introduce a bill granting Asya permanent residency in America. She's a winning child."

"She might be more than that," I said.

"How so?"

"There're hints by my English grandmother, Victoria, who is familiar with British royalty, that Asya could be descended from the last Russian royal family, the Romanov's. Asya is a nickname for Anastasia."

"Their entire family was butchered by the Communists in 1917," my father objected.

"According to persisting rumor, one child was ill and receiving medical treatment elsewhere. Upon recovering, she was smuggled to the West," I said.

"That *would* complicate matters. You have high-level contacts in Moscow. What do you think their attitude would be?" my father asked.

"I can't even guess," I said, shaking my head.

Chapter 76

Our conversation turned to other matters: my oldest sister's wedding plan, my younger sister's life as a Barnard College sophomore, and the persistence of my youngest sister's intention to become a detective. I made anticipated comments as my thoughts traveled along other paths.

Asya's possible Romanov ancestry had thrown me for a loop. Had the Russian government's attitude changed since it murdered the royal family a hundred years ago? Not during the Communist years but these were long gone. My guide in Moscow had spoken of the "new Russia" but had its attitude changed on this matter too? Would Asya be deemed a threat to the political status quo, as were her descendants a century before, or a prized royalty tourist attraction? A good question, I thought, as I hugged my father goodbye.

D.D. saw me that afternoon. Like many retirees, he found retirement painful. His last job had been as a federal prosecutor. Babysitting grandchildren gained hugs but lacked intellectual interest and particularly the intricacy of problems like Asya's. Payment matters came first.

"We want Asya to remain in our family and will cover your fee and expenses. We have financial means so this won't be a problem, The money will be wired into your account today," I said.

This may seem a cold way to begin but our relationship was business and not personal. His government salary had been far below what he might have earned in private practice. D.D. handed me a card with bank wiring instructions and I signed a form designating him as legal advisor. What I now shared would have as great confidentiality as America's legal system could devise, even better than that enjoyed by doctors.

As I spoke, I tried to keep my emotions in check. I had been an adoptee and speaking of Asya's adoption aroused deep feelings. Our talk wasn't only a legal matter for Asya. It was life itself.

Chapter 77

"Asya lived with a diplomat and his wife in Germany before coming to America. She speaks German and I'm teaching her English just as she's improving my German," I said, becoming overcome with emotion.

"There are tissues on the desk. Take your time," D.D. said.

I swallowed, wiped my eyes, and continued.

"Her parents were recently murdered with she hiding as it happened. She's considered a witness by the police though she apparently saw nothing, just hearing screams during their torture. *She* may have been the intended victim," I said.

"Why would anyone want to kill a child?" D.D. asked, frowning.

I swallowed again before answering.

"We're not sure but the answer may lie in Russian history. You know what happened to the last Tsar of the Romanov dynasty?" I asked, though the question was rhetorical.

"He and his family were murdered by the Communists. They considered the existence of any family member to be risky for the new regime which was under attack by Western armies."

Margaret and Randy

"Yes. Well, it may be that Asya, which is the shortened form of Anastasia, is a Romanov descendant. She *is* beautiful but this may be the real reason why she was given the nickname *princess*."

Now it was D.D. who swallowed before smiling.

"You don't bring me simple cases" he said.

"The shrewdest lawyers get the most intricate ones," I said, joining his smile.

One can never flatter too much.

"She's well protected with my family's bodyguard and others on-call."

"You said *parents*. Were they her legal parents?" D.D. asked.

"Not quite. The records seem dicey and the German authorities haven't been cooperative. 'We're checking,' is their latest word," I said.

"Strings are being pulled behind the scene," D.D. speculated.

"I have European contacts. I think it's time for me to pull strings too," I said.

Chapter 78

I felt better after speaking with D.D., as one should after speaking with their lawyer. Not because they've vowed to win your case, which no lawyer can do, but because they appear to know what they're doing and you feel comfortable leaving your problem in their hands.

I phoned my Berlin father (and boss) who has high political contacts.

"The American branch prospers but I have a personal problem, papa," I opened with.

"If it is what I think, I've heard about it from Borya. You should call him. Sorry, but my plane is boarding," he said, abruptly ending the call.

I wasn't completely surprised. Borya, my uncle, is a powerful official in the SVR, Russia's Foreign Intelligence Service. His responsibility is to know *everything*.

"What would be Russia's attitude if an authentic Romanov descendent were discovered?" I asked Borya.

"The president would be pleased and concerned," Borya replied

"Why?" I asked, with surprise.

"Think what Britain's royal family does for that nation's stability and its tourist industry. But because this feeling is not universal, the President is concerned for her safety. She must have been the intended victim, not her unfortunate parents."

"That's what I think too."

"The president wishes a personal evaluation of the child. Would you object to her meeting with our representatives?"

"Of course not," I said immediately, knowing that his courteous request was both a demand and one that would insure Asya's safety.

"Good. They will be traveling on diplomatic passports. One will be a happy surprise. It is your recently married friend who is pregnant. She is nervous and would benefit from the support of an experienced mother."

"When can I expect them?" I asked.

"Within two days since the president considers this matter urgent. The other visitor is revered but kindly and you'll like him They will stay at the Russian Consulate in Manhattan. Would travel into the City be a problem? A car will be sent," Borya said.

"We'll be ready whenever," I said.

"Your children have never visited Moscow and you must bring them. We're family and family is important to Russians," he gently chided.

"Yes, uncle." I said, and our call ended.

Margaret and Randy

It wasn't the first time that I had been scolded about this and wouldn't be the last.

Chapter 79

Borya spoke ambiguously since national intelligence services have long collected electronic signals. I knew who my "recently married friend" was and why she traveled on a diplomatic passport with a phony name and would stay at the Russian Consulate. Page had once been a noted assassin.

After her arrest in New York for a murder inside Berlin's Russian Consulate, she was extradited to Germany for trial. There, feigning innocence and with tears enhanced by her beauty, she had been released and hired by Russia's Intelligence Service. Talented assassins are always needed by governments.

Her accomplice was not as fortunate. After his release on bail he was killed in an alleged street mugging gone wrong. To no one's surprise, his attacker was never found.

Page's mixture of beauty and pollution is as hypnotic as a skyscraper burning, so strange that puzzlement becomes unavoidable. This may be why bad girls often self-destruct and meet nasty ends. Their lack of conviction recoils at their badness as they try to be the sweetheart they long to be.

Having been raped by her father as a child, Page thereafter survived by her wits. First as a high-priced escort and then, propelled by her rage toward men, as an assassin. Money was her narcotic, admiring gold coins soothing her bedtime.

Margaret and Randy

By working undercover and feigning friendship, I enabled Page's arrest in New York, later re-awakening our contact when Moscow began worrying at her acquaintances. The events that followed could scarcely be believed. After Page's involvement in an attempted coup she had been miraculously pardoned. But with the conditions that she marry a pre-selected man to provide the firm control that she needed *and* would immediately become pregnant to permanently change her lifestyle. To my astonishment, Borya insisted on being the child's godfather.

The threat of imminent execution can revise thinking and did with Page. The woman that Asya and I would meet at the consulate had changed from a criminally thin assassin into the anxiety-ridden plumpness of expectancy.

Chapter 80

"We'll be going to New York City tomorrow. Have you been there?" I asked Asya.

"No," she replied, with the normal lack of curiosity of children who are used to adults planning their lives.

"We'll be meeting two people. They have traveled a long way to see you and one is my good friend," I said.

"What should I wear?" Asya asked, this typical female concern.

"We'll find something suitable from what you have. Manhattan is a fashion center. Maybe we'll go shopping afterward," I said.

Asya looked away, apparently deep in thought, before turning back with an unexpected but understandable question.

"Will we be safe?" she asked.

"Perfectly! We'll travel by car and be accompanied by bodyguards. No one will harm you," I promised.

We spent the next hour studying her limited wardrobe. How should she dress? I asked myself. What would potential royalty wear for a critical interview? The clothing of an ordinary child, I decided, as we chose a light green, belted shirt dress with a collar and buttoned front. I didn't think what she wore mattered. If the DNA results were favorable, fashionistas would vie to create her clothes.

The next day, Asya dressed herself early, adding to her outfit my pearl necklace which I'd suggested. She preened when I complimented her appearance.

"My parents took me to receptions," she said, as if to say, I've done this before.

The car, a limousine bearing flags of the Russian Federation, arrived promptly at 10:00AM bearing a driver and bodyguard. Traffic was light and we arrived at the consulate, a mansion on Manhattan's Upper East Side, at 11:20AM. That I check the time indicates my anxiety, I thought.

Once inside we were on Russian territory. Here, Page, with whatever alias she used, would be safe, as would her mysterious companion.

Chapter 81

The New York City consulate of the Russian Federation is on 91ˢᵗ Street off Central Park. It is a five-story, Renaissance style town house that was built in 1903 as a wedding gift for a wealthy, socially prominent bride. I considered this ironic in view of Russia's Communist history.

As our car glided up Madison Avenue I noticed that Asya had fallen asleep and wondered at the source of my anxiety. Was it at meeting Page or fear of Asya being wrenched from my family?

When the car stopped, I gently wakened Asya. She yawned sleepily as we entered the building to be led to a comfortable sitting room on the second floor. Soon after refreshments arrived as did the very-pregnant Page and a tall, plump, white-bearded man. What struck me about his appearance wasn't his dress—a well-tailored black suit—but the ornate silver crucifix that he wore. Page introduced him as the Moscow Patriarch of the Russian Orthodox Church, addressed him as Your Beatitude, and I followed suit.

Asya and I sat silently, waiting for Page or the Archbishop to take the lead. He spoke first, facing me.

"Would it be best for me to speak in German or English?" he asked.

"I have passable German. Asya is fluent in German and has learned English so English might be best," I said.

Margaret and Randy

"So be it. I'm happy to meet you both. Margaret is well-regarded by our country and I have heard of your recent sadness, my child," he said, facing Asya directly.

When she didn't reply, he spoke again.

"How would you like me to address you?" he asked, in a kindly tone.

"We called her Asya before learning her nickname of *princess*," I said.

My remark seemed to stop the clock.

Chapter 82

"Princess," the Archbishop mused aloud.

"It's because she's so pretty," I said quickly, to ease the awkward moment.

All except Asya smiled. She seemed uncomfortable, unsure what to say, and the Archbishop leaned toward her.

"Did you study the history of Russia in school?" he asked.

"I didn't go to school. My mother taught me at home," she said.

"Yes," he said, briefly befuddled before continuing.

"Russia's history shows how great power can tarnish families, conquering natural loyalty and affection. The Romanov dynasty is a tale of a magnificent family that lost its way as the tsar lost his. The title *tsar* comes from the Roman Caesar, a great conqueror who also met a sad ending."

"He was murdered," Asya said.

"Yes, as were many tsars. Yet many were superb statesmen and they produced a soaring culture of which much was beautiful. Can I tell you a story?" he asked.

Asya nodded, seeming enthralled by his gentle voice.

Margaret and Randy

"A German princess married the last tsar in a love match. They were incredibly happy but made bad political judgments that caused the country to have hard times. They were often unable to sleep, being kept awake by the cries of animals outside."

"Day and night, animals make noise when they're frightened. The poor beasts are no different from the rest of God's creations, alone and afraid and telling it to the silent stars," Asya said.

"Do you feel alone and afraid?" the Archbishop asked.

"How could I not? Though being loved, I never knew my real parents. We were a family that was never a family. Do you feel alone too?" Asya asked.

"The clergy is a lonely job and often unrewarding considering the effort involved. But it's my mission and what I must do."

"I wonder what my mission is," Asya murmured, as if speaking to herself.

"That is what we must discover. In Greek, Anastasia means *the one who is reborn*," the Archbishop said.

Margaret and Randy

Chapter 83

"Your mission is what we must uncover," the Archbishop said, as he led her away.

I wondered at his certainly though he evidently knew more. But why was Page sent to America, advanced in pregnancy and needing a false identity?

Then it hit me. Page wasn't sent to evaluate Asya but to spy for Borya, my uncle and her boss at Russia's Foreign Intelligence Service. She owed him her life after plotting against Russia's president.

Then I had another thought: that while the Archbishop knew the DNA results, the decision about Asya wasn't certain with the future of nuclear-armed Russia and the world hanging in the balance. Was Asya intelligent and thoughtful or dull and impulsive? Could the grown-up Asya be trusted to hold a role in Russia and who would be her guardian until then? Randy and me?

"She's a sweet child," Page said, sidling close when we were alone.

"That she is but why are *you* here though I'm happy to see you," I said.

"*You know*," Page said, with her most charming smile.

"As Borya's spy," I said.

Margaret and Randy

"He's preparing for whatever changes occur in Russia's future," Page said.

"When's your due date?" I said, touching her swollen belly.

"Officially next month though Olga seems so anxious to leave that I'm not sure she'll wait," Page said, with an unexpected blush.

"How does Josef feel about having a daughter?" I asked excitedly, he being her husband.

"He's ecstatic, researching girl's names since we first found out," Page said, as her expression darkened.

"What's wrong?" I asked.

"Maybe nothing but maybe everything," she said tearfully.

"We're friends with whatever name you use. I'm here for whatever you need," I said.

Margaret and Randy

Chapter 84

I held Page's hand as she spoke. Whatever phony name she adopted, she would always be *Page* to me.

"One morning, seven months into what seemed my normal pregnancy, I couldn't get my baby to move. Nothing that usually worked did, whether laying on my side to better feel her kicking or drinking juice to awaken her. I forced myself to eat cake thinking what child doesn't like sugar, but this didn't work either. Nearly paralyzed with fear, I went to my obstetrician's office.

"The nurse placed monitors on my belly and I relaxed upon learning that my daughter's heartbeat was okay. But the anxiety returned after the ultrasound tests. Her growth slowed since the last scan two months earlier, the blood flow to her brain seemed *wrong* and no one appeared to know what the problem was.

"By then, Josef had arrived and we both felt suspended in space, having expected a diagnosis and plan but being given neither. My doctor tried to reassure us by saying that pregnancy consists of quirks with two mutually dependent patients, one inside the other. That communication is impossible with the smaller and when having a look-see with an ultrasound machine you are looking at silhouettes. Move the probe slightly and your opinion changes.

"He said that fetal monitoring, following the peaks and valleys of a baby's heart rate, is imperfect and can even be harmful by urging doctors toward Cesarean sections which are perilous for mothers.

"Finally, the doctor said that he didn't know. My daughter could have a genetic disorder or I could have a rare infection or a problem with my placenta, the baby's lifeline. I can't leave the consulate. Can you find a specialist to give me a second opinion here?" Page pleaded.

Chapter 85

I empathized with Page's pain, having sometimes felt helpless during my pregnancy. But what she wanted might be impossible. Highly-trained medical specialists are stingy with their time and don't make home visits. Particularly not with the machines needed to assess the health of a pregnancy. I raised this objection first.

"I'll do what I can but can't see any obstetrician lugging big machines to a home visit," I said.

"I don't need that. I brought my records and just want another expert to explain them. My doctor is nice but young. I'm confused and need help," she repeated.

This information made satisfying her demand easier.

"I'll do what I can," I said, reaching for my phone.

My best friend, Erika, is of a billionaire's family. Their families aren't typical and they get what they want. I called her.

"A good friend has a problem. She's pregnant and wants a second opinion about her condition. She has her medical records and is staying at Manhattan's Russian Consulate, being unable to leave for reasons it would take too long to explain. Do you know a top-notch obstetrician who would be willing to make a house call? I'll pay whatever his fee and a limo will be sent for him," I said.

Margaret and Randy

Erika understood my implicit message: that the "too long to explain" reason couldn't be spoken on the phone.

Her silence caused my concern until she spoke.

"My dad contributes yearly to the Columbia-Presbyterian Medical Center and is on their financial advisory board. He'll make a call and I'll get back to you," Erika said.

She did in ten minutes. This doctor was all that Page could have wished: an obstetrician who had specialized in high-risk deliveries for thirty-six years, had received numerous awards and, she later said, had a gentle voice and comforting manner.

Chapter 86

I sat with Page as Doctor Lindley spoke. Partly to provide support but also to learn since I wanted at least three more babies.

"My doctor said there could be a problem with my placenta. Maybe I have the world's worst Airbnb," Page gushed, trying to lighten her anxiety with humor.

"Relax while I read your records. We'll talk in a few minutes," he said, calmly.

Page stared anxiously, gripping my hand as we sat on the sofa. After ten minutes and several mutters, Doctor Lindley spoke, more like a teacher than a doctor.

"The placenta is a mysterious organ and we still know little what it does. It's a home for your infant within which she gains oxygen and nutrients as she grows. The oxygen slowly reduces so she must be tracked for the ideal moment to get her out, when being born is less scary than staying inside. After studying your records, I very much doubt that your baby is in trouble."

Page teared as Doctor Lindley continued.

"A child's brain measure, their middle cerebral artery Doppler, shows how much resistance there is to blood flowing to the brain. While a higher level of resistance is normal, your baby's low resistance can, theoretically, show what's called a *brain-sparing effect* when a starving baby diverts the little she's getting to essential organs. But this is debatable and there's no agreement what it means. I wouldn't have done this test.

"Growth scans are hazy too. They're like trying to guess someone's weight using their shoe size and height. *My* prediction is that your daughter will be born full-term and healthy, and bankrupt you for clothes and college tuition someday."

Now, Page couldn't hold back the tears.

Chapter 87

Asya's interviews continued. It seemed that choosing a nation's royalty can't be made in an hour or even a day and our trip into the City dragged on into its third day. *Everyone* at the consulate wanted to meet her. Which I would have expected to try her stamina but she handled well. It was as if her parents had prepared her for such eventuality, perhaps hoping that it would occur.

During these days I tried keeping up with my other responsibilities. Face-Timing with my toddlers and their babysitter-bodyguard, Mila, and with Randy to give the support that he required. A mother's major task is to care for everyone in her tribe.

Page attended many of the receptions with Asya, being the adult female who accompanied her where girls need go whenever.

"It's hard to believe she's a child. She speaks to adults as if she were one of them, and without curiosity about the fanfare that one would expect," Page said.

"What do you think their decision will be?" I asked.

"That's above my pay grade but I'll give her a great report to Borya and expect the others will do the same. Then Russia's president decides and where she'll live."

"They might take her from us," I whispered, afraid that speaking it loudly would make this true.

Margaret and Randy

"I wouldn't expect it. She needs a stable, loving family particularly after what she's experienced, one that you're providing. Why change what's working?"

"We can only hope," I murmured.

This decision was above *both* our pay grades.

Chapter 88

I didn't attend Asya's receptions, not being invited and deciding that this was deliberate. Her evaluation was intended to reveal how she behaved when alone and unhelped. Page later said, "She did fantastic. Like a real princess."

Trying to smother my concern about possibly losing her, I phoned Judd to see how things were going and checked with my office assistant too. Both reported no problems.

I also wrote a letter to my toddlers. Encouraging their literacy had been my goal since their infancy, holding them while reading to them. Even in this internet age, children enjoy the surprise of receiving letters. I wrote to them each day that I was away, describing my adventures and asking about theirs, printing these on impressive, heavy-weight consulate stationary. A typical one follows.

"Dear Donna and James,

"I've had to stay in New York City for a few days and miss you terribly but will be home soon. I'm depending on you to take care of your daddy while I'm away. (I expected him to enjoy reading this!)

"New York City is big and your daddy and I will take you there. It has big buildings and many more people than Greenwich. You can take pictures with your phones to show your friends.

Margaret and Randy

"Asya misses you A LOT and will buy books to read to you. We will be home soon and can't wait to hear all that happened while we were away.

"With hugs and kisses from Asya and Mommy."

My phone trilled the moment that I finished writing. Erika was going into labor.

Chapter 89

I didn't get the details of Erika's childbirth until after returning to Greenwich. Pregnant women sometimes have more things to think about than calling their friends, even those they consider sisters. Her delivery, though ultimately fine, didn't proceed as in Lifetime movies which are bloodless and all smiles. Terror pervaded Erika's experience though she had the same wonderfully supportive obstetrician and nurse as me.

The normal anxiety might have latched onto fear originated by Clive's blackmail. Though now over, I knew from experience that trauma doesn't disappear. It lingers in the background, awaiting its opportunity to revive, like the feeling that one gets upon hearing an unexpected noise while walking a dark street.

"Just the *thought* of pushing out a baby makes me frantic," Erika had told me, as she awaited her delivery doomsday with a mixture of desperation and fear. Because of this she had scheduled a C-section, though without her doctor's blessing since she lacked a sound medical reason and the procedure contains risk. But though its date was set, nobody informed her baby who had another plan.

Three days before the C-section, her doctor told her. "Your baby won't wait. You're three centimeters dilated and your cervix is thinning." He suggested she go into labor and, if it was easier than she expected, change her mind about rejecting vaginal delivery.

She listened calmly before saying politely, "It would have to be *really* easy." Erika heard during her childbirth classes that first-time labors are usually hard and long, with the mother feeling like she's gone through an emotional and physical meat grinder at its end.

Early next morning, after peeing and getting back into bed, Erika had a little cramp like when her period began. These repeated every few minutes and got worse over the next hour. She tried denying what was happening until the cramps became so painful that she had to lean against the wall for support.

Her pain got worse on the ride to the hospital, through registration and onto the delivery floor. Despite this, Erika felt calm, believing that her C-section was only minutes away. The nurse was fascinated by her. "You're at seven centimeters with a paper-thin cervix. This is a textbook case of perfect labor. Are you *sure* you don't want vaginal delivery?"

Erika waited to decide until the epidural was working since she would have this pain-killer no matter which delivery method she chose. At that point, feeling she had gotten so far without having a breakdown, she followed her doctor's advice. "I think I can do vaginal delivery," Erika told him.

She did and quickly had a beautiful, wriggling, wet baby in her arms.

Chapter 90

I was a bundle of nerves when we left the consulate though Asya was calm. For her, the previous days had been a round of great food and meeting adults who would listen to her for as long as she chose. No child wants more.

I told her of my promise that she would bring presents to Donna and James so we would stop at a book store before leaving Manhattan, "and shop for clothes if you want." What girl doesn't?

Our first destination was Bergdorf Goodman on West 57th Street, the favored store of Erika who describes herself as "a serious shopper." I wouldn't disagree and we had been there many times.

Asya's choices wouldn't have been mine but I went along with them, a basic parental task being to encourage their child's independence. The clothes were colorful: a red and black, polyester-spandex, polka-dot knit dress with a round neckline, short, puffy sleeves, and an oversized bow at the waist; and a Burberry long puffer coat with belted waist and a hooded collar. Her joy was worth the expense and they would be warm enough for a Russian winter trip too.

I would have liked Asya to see the fantastic views from the store's 7th floor restaurant but we had already tired the patience of the two bodyguards that the consul-general insisted accompany us home.

Margaret and Randy

The Rizzoli Bookstore, on lower Broadway, is another gem. Leaving Manhattan noise, you enter into calmness with peaceful music playing in the background and clearly labelled shelves with paintings above. A bookstore feast for the eyes and escapism for the mind.

I chose *Barnyard Dance, What's Wrong, Little Pookie?* and *But Not The Hippopotamus*. I enjoyed these books during my childhood for they mixed high spirits with high emotions. Taking children's feelings seriously and giving them a language of their own to make speaking of difficult topics easier as by saying, "I'm angry as a duck." These apparently simple books had always felt far from it to me.

Margaret and Randy

Chapter 91

The drive to Greenwich was uneventful and Asya quickly nodded off against my shoulder. After staring out the car window for a few minutes, I too fell asleep, awakening when the car braked at a light near home. The bodyguards smilingly declined my invitation to stay for dinner and left. The house felt empty and was, Mila having taken the children to visit their grandparents.

I suggested that Asya resume her nap and she did, going to her room without protest. The recent events were exhausting and children have limited self-control. Hers had clearly been drained and mine too. Much had happened in a short time.

Being a non-drinking Mormon, I chose hot chocolate in place of whiskey and settled on the couch to read an old paperback, one that I'd found in the back of a closet of my inherited house. Despite its torn cover, crinkling yellowing pages and small print, the fluid writing and exciting plot grabbed my attention.

A British officer, suffering with ulcers after battling the Nazi occupiers of France, had been ordered back to England. There, against medical advice and despite the pain it created, he still drank whiskey. Now, though perhaps being the world's sickest spy, he was sent back to France on a final mission that only he could do: save his spy group and discover the traitor who had betrayed it to the Nazis.

Margaret and Randy

Why did this plot so entrance me, I wondered, before realizing that it was obvious. My career routinely dealt with deception and danger, shocks which I tried to keep from my family. But how long would I succeed? I feared.

Chapter 92

A security manager's work isn't nine-to-five. It's more like being a sports agent whose job doesn't end when the contract is signed. Instead, they must be continually on-call for whatever actual or simply feared emergency happens, for *them* to resolve and not someone else. These duties were in addition to my being a wife and mother.

Our family routine quickly returned. Princess or not, I was determined to keep Asya's life normal. Here, in Greenwich, she would be an all-American child. This was what Asya wanted too. She diligently studied English, read books in English, and watched English-language TV shows, softly repeating the lines.

I thought of hiring a Russian language instructor for her before deciding to await the DNA results. If negative, her nickname of princess would be only that. I could only shrug when Randy asked, "Is she ours?" Knowing that the unsettled situation wasn't fair for any of us and especially not for Asya.

Our love for her deepened as did her intimacy with our children. Losing her would be painful, even if occurring during her adulthood.

What were *her* feelings? I didn't know and didn't ask for they must have been raw since her parents' murder. She would work through their loss throughout her life. Placing the burden of Russia's bloody history on her shoulders would certainly be too much. This was how Randy and I viewed it but we knew that politicians are different.

For James and Donna, Asya was their big sister, playmate, confidante, and buffer against the daily terrors of the grown-up adult world they inhabited. They loved her, she loved them, and we loved them all. What would tomorrow bring? I lay wondering, until the siren awoke us.

"What was *that*?" Randy asked, as I pressed the red button on the night table.

A loud, imposing female voice instantly intruded throughout the house. "An intruder has broken the perimeter. Go to your assigned security location."

Grabbing my robe and pistol, I ran for the children's room.

Margaret and Randy

Chapter 93

The most important lesson that I learned from my sleep-overs at Erika's home was how to keep its occupants safe. Being a billionaire, her father had made security a priority and I followed his example of installing security rooms for residents to wait out danger. Each contains an independent phone line, air, and electrical connection along with a porta-potty, food, weapons, and games to while away time. I expected to find Mila and the children in the second floor chamber and did.

"You handle emergencies calmly," Randy complimented me when this crisis ended.

I smiled but didn't tell him the truth. He would have been astonished to learn that lack of self-confidence was my weakness. But I hung back from saying it, burying this in my innermost being. Rationalizing this reserve by telling myself that it was a poor tactic to expose weakness to those who depended on you for they would then bear danger with less faith.

Once in the security room, I told the children the truth, using simple language so they would understand.

"This room is our safety room, like the cave where a bear hides from danger. When you hear the loud woman's voice, you must run to this room where you will be safe with Mila and me and your daddy. Is that clear?" I asked in a non-pampering, demanding tone, and the three children nodded.

Margaret and Randy

I pointed to the porta-potty in the corner and asked if anyone wanted to use it but none did. While I distributed picture puzzles and coloring supplies to occupy their time, Mila checked the Heckler & Koch forty-round, 7.62X51MM assault rifle and 12-gauge Mossberg Shockwave pump-action shotgun hanging on the wall. Both were contrasts in appearance for the rifle weighs over eleven-pounds while the shotgun, with its "birds head" grip and fourteen-inch barrel, weighs half that. Plenty powerful to confront the fool who would attempt entry, I thought.

Chapter 94

As with earlier such events at Erika's home, this scare was less serious than we feared though it might well have been worse. There had been a home-invasion robbery attempt a mile away with its failure resulting in a shoot-out. Police Sergeant Alamo, a family friend since my childhood, dropped in to check on us and had supplied details after the children were returned to their beds.

"Our Burglary Unit was following the offshoot of a home-invasion crew that we'd put away, a really nasty piece of work. They'd beat people and crack kids violently. Terrify victims by biting off women's nipples and having little girls suck their fathers. Thrust a gun into a woman's groin and say, 'You won't be using this anymore,' or force a gun into a kid's mouth and click the hammer. The rottenest bunch you could find.

"Their scheme was for two guys to come to the house with flowers while the third guy stayed in the car with the motor running. Holding the flowers in front of their faces with nylon stockings rolled up beneath the baseball caps they wore. When they rang the bell, whoever looked through the peephole or cracked the door chain could only see flowers and the glimpse of a face. 'Floral Delivery,' the crook would say and as the victim opened the door, the guys would pull the stockings down over their faces and rush in.

Margaret and Randy

"We'd been following them for months. An informant, who I'd helped get a reduced sentence, told us that the gang had targeted a wealthy surgeon and the score was going down in two days.

"We started setting up the next day, getting heavy firepower into the intended victim's house and one across the street. We invited him to leave but he insisted on staying, saying, "Nobody'll get us out of our home." He and his wife said they'd do whatever we wanted.

"We moved our guys into the house discreetly and, going door-to-door, told neighbors what was happening. The people directly across the street said they wouldn't cooperate and didn't like their neighbor. But the guy next door told us, "You can have anything you want." We put four guys in the target's house, four across the street, and ten spread through the neighborhood.

"We saw the crew pull up with the driver staying behind. As they approached the door, the driver of the getaway car resisted and was shot right away. Our man, holding a machine gun, bravely opened the home's door and said, "Police. Lay down." They said, "Fuck you," opened fire, and ran with our guys chasing them down the street and everyone firing.

"When the car's driver was hit, his foot was on the accelerator and the car went over the lawn, hitting a fire hydrant before reversing and coming back at us. That was when we opened up with hundreds of rounds. Sorry for the disturbance," Sergeant Alamo said sheepishly.

Margaret and Randy

"Did any of these monsters survive?" I asked.

"One did for a while but it took too long to get him to the hospital," he said.

I understood. "There is a justice of lawyers and the courtroom, and a justice of The Prophets and of God," is my company's motto.

Chapter 95

The "Shootout in Posh Greenwich," as one headline put it, got worldwide attention and changed resident behavior. The sale of home alarms and guns skyrocketed but so did local cooperation. People no longer felt safe in their family bubble, accepting the notion that close-by aid could be needed as during Greenwich's frontier day roots.

Another reaction happened here, just like after the 9/11 terror attack that caused three-thousand ordinary Americans to lose their lives. Those without a supportive spouse decided that they wanted one and focused on dating apps for their quest. Even teenagers became affected.

One could once turn to best-selling books for help in traversing the dating landscape. *The Rules: Time-Tested Secrets for Capturing the Heart of Mr. Right* had taught women to let a man take the lead and not rush into sex. But with apps like Match.com and Bumble altering dating, social norms hadn't kept up. New vocabulary emerged to depict the confusing experience of finding a mate: catfishing (creating a false online identity); ghosting (silently ending a relationship by not responding); breadcrumbing (sending coquettish, evasive messages). One app added a panic button so a user could alert a friend if their date was going poorly or they felt at risk of being physically (not just emotionally) hurt. Thus, feeling bewildered (which wasn't new) and unsafe (which was), my nineteen-year-old sister, Melanie, visited. After a quick obligatory greeting, she turned to business.

Margaret and Randy

"I'm looking for a husband," she said.

Feeling mystified, I made a safe response.

"Have you told mom this?" I asked.

"Why? If our family were more religious, I'd have been married five years ago," Melanie said.

This was an exaggeration. Today's Mormons *do not* marry at fourteen, except perhaps within unsanctioned sects. But getting married at nineteen is normal in all cultures though neither Randy nor I had been ready then and marital age has risen in recent decades.

"Okay. How can I help?" I asked, adopting my Big Sister role.

"What's your opinion of the FDS?" Melanie asked earnestly, looking me straight in the eye.

Margaret and Randy

Chapter 96

Surviving motherhood requires learning many things but not about secret societies. Was the FDS one of these, I wondered.

"I've never heard of the FDS," I admitted.

This *wasn't* the response that my younger sister wanted. A Big Sister *is* expected to know!

After a roll of her eyes and giving me a "look," Melanie began her explanation.

"You know what Reddit is, don't you?" she asked, failing to conceal her frustration.

"An internet discussion site?" I replied, feeling hesitantly confident.

"Yes, and one of its conversations concerns Female Dating Strategy or FDS."

"That's sounds innocent," I said, instantly relieved that she hadn't become emotionally imprisoned by a weird cult. One can never be sure with teenagers.

Melanie again rolled her eyes as I became the sympathetic Big Sister she needed.

"What *exactly* is it?" I asked, with real interest. While my marriage seemed sturdy, no wife can ever be one-hundred-percent certain.

Margaret and Randy

"It's a good group," Melanie said, in a more relaxed tone before continuing. "Members around the world tell of their dates and divorces and sex lives. There's even an FDS Handbook advising women to not have sex before commitment and to assess men pitilessly. That a woman should cut off men who add no value to her life. Like those who lie about wanting a serious relationship but only want sex, which we call *future-faking*, or aren't financially independent adults."

"That's good advice. Every woman should follow it!" I said, with real enthusiasm.

"Yes but the forum also makes demands of women. That what is asked of men must be practiced by women too."

"Hmm," I mused.

"The problem is that everyone lies in online dating, telling only some truths about themselves with women typically lying about their weight and men about their height.."

"A dreamier posting probably receives more responses," I said, neutrally.

"That's what the FDS Handbook said and why the site is needed: to arm its women warriors on the uncultured dating scene."

The older generation sometimes learn from the younger, I thought approvingly.

Margaret and Randy

Chapter 97

My adoptive father, who was a highly respected lawyer before being elected a judge, once advised me about worrying. "Being a worrier is good since it forces you to do your best. Would you choose a doctor or lawyer who didn't worry?" he asked.

"No," I replied.

"Yes, so try to adopt my *Worry Rule*: every morning, sit down and worry for ten minutes as much as you want. Then just do your best since the only true failure is never trying."

I practiced this thereafter and it helped, though less after becoming a mother when fretting seemed to become a full-time job, and one which increased after Asya joined our family.

Though undemanding and exuding gentility (her parents had obviously raised her well), the scope of her life multiplied after her DNA was found to match the Romanov. Thereafter, her welfare became the interest of nations.

Bureaucrats worked speedily and her German citizenship and American legal residence were quickly approved. Nor did the Russian Federation raise concern until Greenwich's shootout lifted the town's profile to stratospheric height.

Formerly viewed as a boring town occupied by wealthy executives, it now became considered as sister city to Kabul, lacking only their suicide bombings. My first indication of this came in a phone call from Moscow.

"Thank you for helping Page," Uncle Borya said, without preamble.

Being a high ranking official of the SVR (*Sluzhba Vneshney Razvedki*), Russia's Foreign Intelligence Service, this hard warrior, ensnared in a buzzsaw of Machiavellian events, didn't waste words.

"I care about her and was glad to do it," I said.

"You must bring your children to Moscow. They should get to know their motherland," he said, in a mock chiding tone.

"I will. I promise. When they're a bit older, during a summer," I said, closing this topic.

Visiting Russia with my family was a recurring issue so I wondered why he really called. Borya isn't a "thank you" kind of person though being considered jolly by my kids who treasure his elaborate presents.

"Our president called me, He is concerned for Asya's safety," Borya said.

So *this* is why he phoned, I told myself, and tried to form an acceptable response.

Chapter 98

"Greenwich is safe, not murder-laden Chicago," I insisted.

"I know but the president is being pressured. He needs something," Borya said

The silence lengthened until an idea popped into my mind.

"What about this? I'll increase the number of motion detectors around my house and have an additional live-in bodyguard. The house opposite mine is for sale. It could be bought to house Russian diplomats and guards and I'm sure the local police would increase their patrols," I said, knowing that political pressure could arrange it.

I waited anxiously as Borya considered.

"Those are good ideas. I'll suggest them to the president," he said finally.

"Moving Asya wouldn't be healthy considering the trauma she's experienced. We've grown to love her and she's expressed fear of being pulled away," I said, bolstering my case.

"There is that too. We've gotten good reports about her," Borya conceded.

Margaret and Randy

Silence again descended over our conversation as he thought.

"It should be fine. I'll speak with the president. Now you're heading a *royal* household," he said, playfully.

"They're all just kids," I said, casually.

That afternoon I received an E-mail from Randy, having already begun worrying at his likely reaction upon learning we would have *another* live-in bodyguard.

"Darling, I'm not good at writing so don't know what to say except that I love you and long to see you. I don't want to write about the business things I'm doing in Washington and am sure you wouldn't want to read them. I can't find words as easily as you to put down what I feel. This is something else you'll have to teach me. All I want is to write *I love you* over and over. All my love from tip to toe."

With this, I stopped worrying that day.

Chapter 99

Randy was calm after learning of our second live-in bodyguard.

"One with big breasts I hope," he said, with a smile.

Though not being as flat chested as before giving birth, I simply gave him a "look" and asked how his business trip went.

"Well, but I've become less obsessed with those things. My family and community duties now seem most important, to reap the joy from living an honorable life," he said.

Feeling stunned by this philosophical outburst from a coldly scientific person, I just stared as he continued.

"I've realized that self-control is important too. Like not pushing people when trying to persuade them but instead removing the barriers to our agreement. I'd been getting resistance from DARPA (Defense Advanced Research Projects Agency) to my proposal. They couldn't grasp its benefits but now instead of pushing them and getting nowhere, I added a catalyst."

"A catalyst?" I questioned, knowing its chemistry meaning of a compound that causes change but doesn't enter into it, never having heard the term used when referring to people before.

Margaret and Randy

"Yes, instead of giving more facts and reasons, I looked for the hidden obstacles preventing change and reducing them.

"People like to feel they're in control, not that they're being forced to do something. I pointed out the difference between what they said they wanted to do and were doing, and that staying as things are isn't cost-free. That it would be cheaper and better to change and the needed change wasn't great.

"I also let them try our new product for nothing, not just *telling* them that it's better, and got others to verify what I said. So I learned that achieving change isn't about pushing harder but reducing the barriers to action. Any person's behavior can be changed by doing this," Randy concluded.

"Did you think all this up?" I asked, feeling stunned by the insight.

"Yes. It hit me one morning when I woke up."

"Did I ever say you have a wonderful mind?" I asked.

"I don't remember but I'd rather you said that you love my body," Randy said, grabbing me.

Margaret and Randy

Chapter 100

While showering together, Randy asked, "How are Judd and Ada doing?"

"Okay, I guess," I replied, instantly feeling guilty about not having checked with them for a week.

Combining work with parenting can raise gaps with both, I was learning.

"I'll have to visit them," I said.

Lessening my guilt with the thought that their bodyguards would have contacted me if there were a problem. Which is like telling yourself that your kids are okay because you hear no screaming and wasn't convincing at all.

"I hate when you're away," I said, re-turning my attention to Randy as he soaped my back.

"I won't for a while. The big tech conferences were cancelled because of the coronavirus scare. There'll be no travel until it's better understood," he said.

"Hmm," I responded, closing my eyes and relaxing against him.

"The sudden change is surprising. The stock market soaring and then crashing for what seems like no good reason. Apparently this virus causes cold-like symptoms with most recovering quickly without treatment," I said.

Margaret and Randy

"That's not true according to my dad," Randy said.

"Huh? How do you mean?" I asked, for his surgeon-father was more knowledgeable than either of us.

"Coronavirus *is* scary, though not to all. Those under ten and especially infants seem untouched by it but those with medical issues can be hard hit. An ordinary cold infects the nose, sinuses and throat but COVID-19 can spread to the lungs causing pneumonia. It can destroy kidney cells, beginning a lethal chain reaction with multiple organs failing.

"It's important to enjoy life while we can though people can get afraid when things seem too good, as if feeling they don't deserve it. Have we been shaken financially?" he asked, casually.

As with many couples, I handled our finances along with other family chores.

"I'm almost afraid to say but we're doing better than ever. Investors are fleeing to safe assets like government bonds which is where most of our savings are parked. Money won't be one of our worries," I said.

Later, still relaxed by our closeness and Randy's announcement that he'd be working from home, I went to the safe house to check on Judd and Ada. A glance would have raised anyone's concern.

Chapter 101

An ambulance was parked at the door. Not another shooting, I prayed, as I entered.

In the living room, Judd lay on the sofa surrounded by two Emergency Medical Service workers. Ada approached me as they unfastened the blood pressure cuff from his arm.

"Is it serious?" I asked, with concern.

She took me aside before speaking.

"Not in the usual sense. They said extreme anxiety caused heart palpitation. Now, his blood pressure is normal but I don't know how much more he can take. His parents' lives have been threatened unless he provides the Egmont log-in credential to the murderer and the hard part is that Judd now remembers how to get it."

With all that had been happening, it took a while for me to remember what brought Judd and Ada into my care.

He and Jackson, his murdered co-worker, were investigating rumored problems in the Egmont Group, a network of national financial intelligence units that provides a secure internet system through which members share information about money laundering, the financing of terrorism, tax fraud, and other crimes. Members were required to exchange information through channels of security equal to those of the Egmont Secure Web.

Margaret and Randy

Judd and Jackson had been comparing those having access to when these were used and the files that were opened, correlating these to identify the hackers. Having Egmont data would enable them to crash the system and be like leaving a bank's door open at night.

"I see why his blood pressure hit the roof," I said.

"Well, what do you plan to do about it?" Ada asked, looking at me steadily.

Chapter 102

Once the medical workers left I sat beside Judd.

"How do you feel?" I asked.

"Better after learning that my heart palpitation was only anxiety," he said.

"Severe anxiety can be bad. I've had it and wouldn't knock it," I said, sympathetically.

"What did you do about it?"

"I was told that anxiety happens when a perceived threat arises. Whether it's unreal like when hearing a sudden noise while walking a deserted street or real when being confronted by a mugger. That I need distinguish the few real dangers from the many fantasied ones."

"That sounds like good advice. So what do we do?" he asked.

That Judd said "we" indicated he still trusted my judgment.

"Tell me what happened," I said.

"My father received a threatening phone call saying they would meet Jackson's fate unless I provided the Egmont log-in credential and that instructions would follow."

"What did the police say when you told them?" I asked.

"Only that they're investigating."

"Had they placed a tap on your parents' phone?" I asked.

"I don't think so. If they did, they didn't tell them."

It should have been done, I thought, with my layman's view.

"I'm feeling paranoid," Judd said.

"It's not being paranoid when a killer is around," I said.

My face remained impassive even as rage enveloped me, later realizing that it was caused by the threat made to Judd's parents. Adoptees (like me) revere families.

"I wouldn't trust anything they say. Having already killed, more murders wouldn't matter," I said.

"What should I do when they send the instructions?" Judd asked.

"Tell me and the police. I'll find out what they know," I said.

"They won't tell you anything," Judd said.

"I have my ways," I said, and hoped they would work.

Chapter 103

"A nation that doesn't protect its citizens has begun to die," insisted a long past American presidential candidate. This quote, from a high school history class, seeped into my mind as my rescue plan for Judd formed.

"Have you been in touch with Lincoln since leaving Yale?" I asked Randy.

"We text occasionally. I tried hiring him but he's too much a loner to work within a company atmosphere though he may be changing. His last note mentioned a girlfriend. Why?"" Randy asked, with a puzzled look.

"I need a hacker. He'll be working on the side of the angels and I'll pay twenty-five-thousand-dollars for possibly just a few hours work. Obviously, he must keep his mouth shut," I said.

"That's no trouble. He's socially challenged and buying coffee is a problem for him," Randy said.

"Is he that good a hacker?"

"Better than me," Randy said firmly.

Randy is considered gifted so his compliment was high praise.

"How soon can you reach him?" I asked.

Margaret and Randy

"I have his number. How do you want to handle this?" Randy asked.

"Say that you've been offered a well-paid hacking job but have no time for it. If he's interested, you'll give his number to the contact," I said.

"You're using a cutout to keep us out of it," Randy noted.

"What we're doing isn't kosher," I admitted.

"It sounds very unkosher but you say it'll be on the side of angels?" Randy asked.

"And every good government too!" I said forcefully.

Chapter 104

As Randy later confided, Lincoln's troubled life indicated that if a hacking job was challenging enough, he'd do it for nothing. Bored by high school, he learned hacking in internet chat rooms, then defacing government web sites for fun. When arrested, still a juvenile, he was sentenced to counseling and probation.

Shortly after his eighteenth birthday, as he watched *The Lion King* with his young sister, federal agents burst into his home, scooping up his computer and notes. Lincoln hacked into an American military website in Germany and, from it, sent a bomb threat to his school to close it. Rather than attending school, he favored watching movies and smoking pot.

This time, no longer a youthful offender, he was tried as an adult and given a two-year jail term. After his release on probation, now barred from using a computer or other than a land-line phone, he worked in dreary restaurant jobs until being rescued by a start-up guru who heard of his genius. This tycoon, who had also been a delinquent youth, secured Lincoln's college admission and paid for his education.

After graduating college with help from understanding teachers, Lincoln supported himself with at-home consulting jobs since working within the confines of an office was painful. Mine would be his best paid gig: hacking into government files to learn what was known about the murders.

Margaret and Randy

Lincoln turned out to be as good a hacker as Randy said, gaining the information that I needed within four days. As bonus, I sent him and his girlfriend to explore London for a week, with ten-thousand-dollars for spending money. Randy described her as a sweet, noticeably quiet nurse who Lincoln met at a doc-in-the-box when suffering a sprained ankle. "She's socially challenged too," Randy said.

Three men with long-criminal records were being minimally watched by the staff-strapped police. The government's belief that they lacked enough evidence to permit bugging their phones hadn't stopped Lincoln from doing it.

During conversations that we recorded, the earlier killings and their intention to kill Judd once he delivered were discussed. They would kill Ada too. I also learned the name of the European contact who hired them for this job.

I reached for my phone to call Uncle Borya, to collect on the favor that he owed me.

Chapter 105

Borya is a powerful Russian intelligence officer, as his nickname of *Lucifer* (The Devil) indicates. He is also my cherished uncle who, along with my Russian father, always reminds me of the importance of family. And, like I said, he owed me a favor. Months before, he recruited me for a successful undercover operation in Moscow which just might have saved the Russian president's life and civilization too. Though sounding grandiose, this is accurate. Facts can be stranger than fiction.

Uncle Borya had given me two phone numbers. One, he swears, will raise him from his grave. The other, answered by his chief assistant, was the one I used and she put me through immediately.

"*Sladkiy*" (sweet one), Borya erupted.

"Uncle, I need a favor," I said, coming to the point quickly.

Though jolly when meeting family, Borya isn't into chitchat from his busy office.

"I need two operatives to deal with problematic people. Each agent will be paid twenty-five-thousand-dollars plus expenses and I'll arrange for private transportation. I'll even throw in vacation money for later," I added, though thinking that I might be becoming *too* generous with my client's money. Still, as Judd said, what price is one's life worth?

Margaret and Randy

"I'm sure we can handle that. Are you safe?" he asked.

I sensed the concern in his voice.

"Perfectly. I'm unknown to the targets. They're killers and it's to save lives," I said.

"Will do. How soon will your plane arrive?" Borya asked.

"Will tomorrow morning be too soon?" I asked.

"Not for a favorite of our president or my beloved niece," he said.

"And you wonder why I love you," I said.

Chapter 106

Before beginning an operation, every spy service creates an *EEI*, a file containing the *Essential Elements of Intelligence* or what it needs to know about a particular target. This meant, for me, the murderers' identity, location, and habits. When each left the residence, where they went, even when they showered if possible. Everything!

The agents that Borya was sending were professionals and would expect this. Moreover, I didn't want to waste time collecting it, needing their mission to be quickly completed and for them to leave the country as soon as possible. From our telephone taps and information gained from the police surveillance, I managed to gather this critical information.

Next morning, Sasha and Alyosha arrived at the safe house. I had told the housekeeper to prepare their rooms and for Judd's bodyguards to expect them. Both were tall, spare, blond, blue-eyed, and spoke unaccented English. Which wasn't surprising upon learning that both spent their childhoods in Washington and London. What did surprise me was that they were cousins.

"He's the better looking," Alyosha said, with a warm smile that caused me to like them immediately.

But can I be confident in their skill? I asked myself. Sasha's story over breakfast convinced me that I could.

Margaret and Randy

A financial backer of Islamic terrorists, an avid sailor, was designated for killing using a missile-firing drone that would hone in on a beacon attached to his sailboat. Deniability was needed since this sensitive operation would occur in a friendly country. The beacon was painted to blend with the boat's surface and smeared with a slow-dissolving adhesive in case the mission was canceled. The task of attaching it was given to the two cousins.

They had moved quietly at the port, as they would if approaching a town held by unfriendly forces. Stopping where the boat was tied, they prepared the beacon. When ready, Alyosha put on swim goggles, grabbed his flashlight, and headed for the stern line.

If caught during the operation, they had prepared a convincing story. After drinking with sailors, Alyosha fell into the water and Sasha was trying to pull him out with a rope he found on the dock. To support this story they had carried a bottle of Scotch, drinking it to celebrate their success while walking back to their hotel.

Chapter 107

While I shared the facts that Lincoln's hacking had gathered, Sasha and Alyosha said little, listened to everything, and missed nothing.

"A piece of cake. Is this a rush job?" Alyosha asked.

I relaxed into the sofa.

"As soon as possible and it would be best if it were made to look accidental. Greenwich has earned too many headlines recently," I said, and he nodded.

"One more thing," I said.

They looked at me expectantly.

"After leaving America, if you could similarly handle their contact in Berlin, you'll each receive an additional fifty-thousand dollars. Afterward, you can instruct the pilot to fly you anywhere you'd like to vacation before taking you home," I said.

"You're very generous," Sasha sputtered, almost speechless.

"What is the value of a life?" I said, repeating Judd's words.

Contrary to popular belief, spy agencies are typical bureaucracies with the wages of undercover agents being at the lower end of the pecking order.

Margaret and Randy

Alyosha sang in a slow croon, "Two in the belly and one in the head. Knocks a man down and kills him dead."

Sasha smiled at my puzzled look. "My cousin wants to be an American cowboy," he said.

Five days later, I met anxious looks from Judd and Ada.

"You're safe. You can return home or go wherever you want," I told them.

"Are you sure? *Really* sure?" Ada asked.

Living under threat, even if ultimately unharmed, leaves a mark.

As answer, I showed them a story in the local newspaper. Its headline read, "Three Men Killed in Car Crash. Speed and Alcohol Considered Factors."

Judd held the paper as both read.

"The car went over a cliff and burst into flames," he said."

"A meth lab will be found in their house. I doubt the police will look further," I said, coolly.

Margaret and Randy

Chapter 108

Evidence that people don't always behave rationally can be seen by my choice of career. I hadn't needed to work. Randy, a computer genius, would have happily supported me as a stay-at-home mother. He would always earn enough to support our family and the fortune that we robbed from a German crook several years before lay in foreign accounts under *my* control. Though feeling confident of Randy's affection, I wasn't a fool and knew of failed relationships.

So, not needing to work, why do I? For the same mysterious reason that a person will jump into a thundering current to rescue a drowning animal: for its own sake. But maybe for the challenge too since, above all, because I feel that I must!

I had survived terrifying situations and now battle for others whose plight moves me. Like the blackmail of Erika and the dangers that Judd and Ada faced, which were now ended.

But family is important too, I reminded myself and not for the first time. All go through childhood wondering who their parents are when not being Mom or Dad. For this reason some children eavesdrop or secretly rummage through dresser drawers. Determined not to be a stranger to my children, I removed my invisible manager's cap as I entered my home, seeking my children for talking time which they would consider mere play.

Chapter 109

James and Donna were in Asya's bedroom. While James played a video game, Asya helped Donna do a Princess picture puzzle as Mila, one of their two bodyguards, looked on. Like any nanny except for her concealed Glock.

"How is everyone?" I asked cheerily, if too loudly.

Donna and James smiled before returning to their activities. Asya said, "well," in a stiff, adult-like tone. The death of one's parents doesn't lead to quick recovery or much playfulness. Still, the courage to dare and dream are the greatest gifts that a parent can give their children and I intended these for mine.

"Where were you?" Asya asked, sounding upset.

I understood. I represent her security and she's asking because she's afraid. It's time that I gave a vital lesson to all three.

"Have I ever told you the kind of work I do?" I asked.

Being the oldest, Asya replied for all, "No."

"I run a business that protects people who are afraid," I began.

"Why are they afraid?" she asked.

"Because people want to hurt them. My business protects them so they need no longer be afraid," I said.

Margaret and Randy

I let my statement sink in before continuing. Mila listened too.

"Worrying about danger is built into our nerves. Thousands of years ago, people were threatened by tigers. So now whenever we sense danger, we routinely tell ourselves: *that's a tiger*, though it might be a rabbit. Almost all of our worries turn out to be like friendly bunnies and not dangerous tigers. Your mommy protects people from the tigers. Is that clear?" I asked.

I feared that my lesson might have been above my toddlers' level of maturity but it wasn't. James and Donna looked as serious as young children can and Asya nodded her head.

"Good! Now would you like the chocolate-peanut butter cookies that grandma brought over?" I asked, with a big smile.

Serious-minded time was over.

Margaret and Randy

Chapter 110

While James and Donna attended a Montessori preschool and Asya was privately tutored at home, I did my never-ending paperwork.

Every business is a bureaucracy and providing security most of all. When people's lives are at stake, *everything* must be documented for if tragedy happens, unwelcome greedy lawyers quickly arrive.

So I was glad for the break when Erika invited me to her step-mother's birthday. It was to be an all adult scene with no children allowed.

"But bring Asya. My dad would like to meet her," Erika said.

"Okay," I said, pondering this.

"One of his companies is investing in Siberia," she added.

This explained it! Obviously, Erika had told her father about Asya. As partner of a hedge fund, he was always on the lookout for those who could aid his investments. Not Asya directly but, like they say, it's often not what you know but who you know that counts and Asya would be meeting them.

The party's location, at Manhattan's famed Russian Tea Room, surprised me. I had been there before and loved it but Erika's father was American. Then I remembered that his present (second) wife, Sara, was born in Russia though brought up by Finnish adoptive parents.

"Would you like to go to a birthday party?" I asked Asya.

Even now, though only ten, she wasn't a child to order around. She didn't answer immediately, as if awaiting more information.

"It's at a famous Russian restaurant in Manhattan," I said.

The word "Russian" seemed to convince her.

Margaret and Randy

Chapter 111

The Russian Tea Room is a Manhattan icon. Located down the street from Carnegie Music Hall, it serves the best Russian dishes of Chicken Kiev, Beef Stroganoff (noodles with beef), and Borscht (beet soup) in the city along with exotic entrees like cocoa-dusted seared venison with truffle-scented cheese dumplings. Its décor, with original artwork by Picasso and Chagall and a giant crystal-like water-filled sculpture of a bear filled with fish, is unique for a restaurant.

That night we were a party of eight: Erika's father, Hamilton (call me "Harry") and his wife, Sara; Erika and her fiancée, Clarence; Asya and me; and Harry's business associate, Joseph, and his wife, Alison.

Erika's step-brother and step-sisters were visiting family in Finland and my husband, Randy, was at home caring for our children. Though mannerly, he's not a social person and dislikes parties. I used the excuse that he had just returned from a business trip, was shortly leaving on another, and needed time with our children though this wasn't required. Erika and her family tolerate Randy's ways. They also know that, were a crisis to develop, he would back them to the end.

Joseph, a tall, bearded man in his fifties who managed Harry's European affairs, sat silently as his second trophy wife, Alison, bubbled on about a celebrity party they recently attended.

Margaret and Randy

Being a healthy-foodie and semi-vegetarian, eating out is often a problem where meat is considered king. But at the Russian Tea Room I had always managed to eat to my taste, usually salmon, rice, vegetables, and bread. With, as finale, the rich chocolate mousse which is to die for though Erika insisted that the cherry crepes with chilled raspberry vodka beat anything.

Conversation turned to the usual chit-chat of Greenwich events and family matters until Alison interrupted. Turning to her husband she said, "Tell them why you stopped reading fortunes." Then, looking at us, she added, "It's like something out of a horror movie."

Margaret and Randy

Chapter 112

Joseph's appearance was so categorically of an English gentleman that it came as no surprise when Erika later told me that he was born in Boston. His studied silence was joined by an annoyed stare at his wife after she spoke. Her beauty wasn't matched by intuition but that obviously wasn't why he married her.

"Oh, do tell them," she pleaded again, with the tone of a child begging for a favored sweet.

Finally, after a forced smile, he did.

"Thirty years ago, I was introduced to palm reading by a painting: *The Fortune Teller* by Enrique Simonet. It hangs in my library and worth ten times what I paid," Joseph began.

Harry, a fellow investor, nodded approval as Joseph continued.

"The subject interested me and I did some study. Palmistry, palm-reading, claims to foretell the future through studying the palm. It's practiced by the highest Hindu caste and discussed in the Hebrew Bible though being viewed as phony by academics.

"In reading the palm one focuses on its various *lines* such as the *heart line* or *life line* and *mounts* or *bumps*. Also the characteristics of the fingers, skin texture and color, shape of the palm, and flexibility of the hand.

Margaret and Randy

"The palmist first reads the person's dominant hand, that which they use most. It's considered to represent the conscious mind with the other hand representing hidden hereditary traits and their past-life or *karmic* condition."

Asya, though outwardly bored by the past chit-chat, seemed to awaken and stared fixedly at Joseph.

"As a teenager, I foretold events using the popular Ouija Board, adding my mix to get girlfriends," he said, with a smile.

"But you were very good at it. Tell them why you stopped telling fortunes!" Alison repeated, as if being unable to wait for the punch line of a previously heard joke.

But it wasn't a joke that we heard.

Chapter 113

"You know those parties where people do stupid things for fun?" Joseph asked rhetorically, before continuing.

"Well, it happened at a society shindig at Gregory's townhouse. His wife is into the occult and she'd hired a tarot reader. I never believed in cartomancy, which is what it's scholarly called, but all agreed so there was no polite way I could refuse."

"What are tarot cards?" Harry asked.

Joseph leaned back in his chair and adopted an academic tone. Despite his investment skill, he had scholarly interests. Erika later told me that he had wanted to be a history teacher but couldn't make a good living that way.

"The belief in fortune-telling using tarot cards began with 18th century French Protestant clerics and royalty who believed that the cards derived from ancient mythology. The word *tarot* comes from the Egyptian word t*ar* meaning *path* and the word *ro* or *rog* means *king* or *royal*. Tarot cards were linked to the Egyptian Book of Thoth though there's no evidence of this.

"Since then its twenty-one cards have been used by gypsies to tell fortunes and by Jungian psychologists to tap into the unconscious with its pictures of a Man Hung Up by the Feet, the Wheel of Fortunc, or the Tower Struck by Lightning. Card interpretations are intended for spiritual growth in response to particular questions: Is there a pattern to the situations I face? Is a present event related to something in the past. The goals are for greater peace of mind and a strengthening of the deepest self."

"Surely no one could dispute these," Erika said.

"Yes, if tarot reading worked," Joseph said.

"It told the truth about you," Alison stressed.

Her angry tone aroused my thought that Joseph's mind might be on Trophy Wife Number Three.

Chapter 114

We stared at Joseph as he began his story.

"Our tarot reader, Lady Zelda she called herself, looked the part being tall with flaming red hair. Mine was the last fortune to be read and I'd listened to the others with little interest, not believing in cartomancy.

"Before beginning, she gave an introductory spiel. She said the future is fluid so positive predictions are impossible. Instead, she would identify *possible* outcomes for a person and examine influences related to it. She said her task was to provide more information so better choices could be made but that she could not guarantee an outcome.

"My reading went like the others. The cards were dealt in an arrangement called a *spread*. Mine was The Three Fates with the first card representing the past, the second indicating the present, and the third signifying the future.

"My first card was *The Magician*. It shows a man standing in front of his powerful altar with tools representing the four directions. Its message was that I must tap into my full potential rather than hold back, that new beginnings and opportunities would arise.

"My second card was *The Fool* who, despite its name, is the wisest person who knows everything. It symbolizes the immortal spirit and insight, a new cycle of trust and innocence from the inner child.

Margaret and Randy

"My last card was *The Wheel of Fortune* which shows a revolving wheel embodying the Wheel of Life. In each corner are four winged creatures seated upon clouds. It signaled that a change of fortune was coming to my life."

"As it did since your investments flourished," Harry interjected.

Another person might have said, "You became a billionaire," but Harry didn't. Extremely wealthy people don't talk about money.

Chapter 115

"I stopped telling fortunes after getting too good at it, having told one that was *too* accurate. It was Trevor's. You know what happened, Harry," Joseph said.

"Yes. He killed himself," Harry agreed.

"I'd told his fortune two days earlier, relaxing after dinner, talking about nothing important as old friends do. I decided to give it a try, not having done it in years.

"In studying the ridges and bumps of his hand, I read his looming death. Yet he looked healthy and so far as I knew had no medical problems. He wasn't into risky sports and avoided travel, being a home-body. But his hand told me that he would die. Not wanting to tell him this, I said what everyone wants to hear: that he has great talent and would have a happy life.

"Though trying not to think about what I'd seen, I couldn't sleep that night. Even after assuring myself that fortune tellers are fakes and had I collected a fee I could be indicted for fraud since Trevor was healthy and lived a temperate life. The market upheaval had captured my attention until you phoned to tell me that Trevor hanged himself," Joseph said, turning to Harry.

"Yes," Harry said, solemnly.

"That's why I've never told another fortune," Joseph said.

Margaret and Randy

It *is* like a horror movie, I thought, as I looked into the stunned faces. Only Asya stayed calm.

"Tell my fortune, please" she said, handing him her palm.

Chapter 116

Joseph didn't immediately respond to Asya's request. Looking baffled and wanting to refuse but also to not hurt her feelings.

"I'm afraid that what I say might upset you," he said honestly.

"My parents were murdered and assassins seek me. What greater pain could befall me?" she asked.

Joseph looked at the rest of us, seeking a gentle way out. But none of us spoke since there was none. He slowly reached for Asya's hand.

As he studied it, the distress left his face to be replaced by absorption.

"I see troubles in your hand but these have gone. While many enemies await their chance, you now have powerful allies. America will not be your only home. When grown, you will travel to a land where vast crowds and a husband await you, and you will have many children," Joseph said.

I felt like laughing from relief but controlled myself.

"With all my enemies, will I have a long life?" Asya asked.

"You will live unto generations but be in constant danger from treachery and cowardice. You will have a mighty guardian though who they are I cannot see," Joseph answered, speaking in almost Biblical tones.

Asya stared at her palm before replacing it in her lap, then looking beyond us into the distance. She seemed unfocused and might have been peering within. Then her eyes caught mine and my heart sang with joy though her words shocked me.

"I have my mother. If I ever need someone to watch my ass, I know who to call."

Now where had she heard *that* line? I wondered.

Chapter 117

The next morning I asked Asya, "How did you sleep?"

"I sleep good," she said.

My mothering instinct got the best of me.

"I slept well," I said gently.

Being a conscientious student, Asya readily accepted my correction.

"I slept well," she repeated, then adding, "and had no need for cheery dreams."

She's sturdy, I thought, but it's time for her to return to being a child.

"What would you like to do today?" I asked.

"Stay with you."

"I have to go into the office today," I said.

"That's okay. I'll go with you," she said, practicing her assertiveness and American slang.

I immediately agreed though whether from over-protectiveness or feeling that it would give her a helpful education I wasn't sure. Certainly, we were both glad to leave the house.

Margaret and Randy

It was at the beginning of the pandemic panic with people in Connecticut being ordered to shelter in place. But essential businesses were exempt which included security companies. From caution, all my employees had been tested for this virus and were found to be negative. Moreover, none were in what was considered a particularly vulnerable group as being elderly.

My two office workers, Jordan and his wife, Elizabeth, awaited us when I arrived with Asya and her bodyguard at the office overlooking Greenwich Harbor.

Despite the informality which I strove to maintain, corporate guidelines were strict. These required a monthly meeting during which the previous month's activities were recorded along with new business. The Chief Accountant in Berlin was a stickler and I heard about missing commas!

Asya played an essential role at that meeting. Elizabeth had just given birth and Asya was assigned to watch the baby, Holly, as she lay on the sofa. It was good training for her "many children" that Joseph had predicted.

Margaret and Randy

Chapter 118

Even with a conscientious babysitter, a parent shouldn't remove attention from their baby for long. Thus, as we spoke, Elizabeth and I periodically turned toward Holly who was delightedly exchanging baby faces and murmurs with Asya.

She'll be a great mother, I thought.

"So, what's been going on?" I asked, turning toward Jordan.

"We've been offered a *very* well-paying job but I wanted to talk to you before contracting for it," Jordan said.

"Why?" I asked, expecting my employees to behave independently.

"It's *tricky*," he said slowly.

Asya listened as she stuck out her tongue toward the squealing Holly.

"It's a rescue of sorts."

"We've always done rescues," I said.

"Of sorts," Jordan repeated.

I waited.

"You know about Leroy King."

Margaret and Randy

"Of course," I said.

King's trouble was a hot news item. His billions were earned through high-flying investments. Deals have winners and losers and losers don't always take their losses well.

King had bet against the stock of a company owned by Venezuelan officials and won. Which meant they had lost and so did King, who was quickly arrested on phony charges and awaited trial. As everyone knew, the jury's belief was beside the point. King was considered guilty by the government and this is what counted. A long prison sentence was expected.

"And the job that has been offered us?" I asked rhetorically.

"To bring this American home to his family," Jordan said.

That had a nice ring for me.

Chapter 119

"Where is King now?" I asked.

"He's out on bail, prisoner in a house in Venezuela. Forbidden contact with his lawyer, or with his wife who flew from New York to be with him. Apart from higher blood pressure he's alright but depressed."

"I wouldn't expect otherwise," I said, sympathetically.

"We're been offered twenty-five-million-dollars to bring him home," Jordan said.

"That's a princely sum."

"He's a financial prince but the job won't be easy. His house is guarded around-the-clock," Jordan said.

"Assuming that the guards can't be bribed, I see only two alternatives," I said, looking directly at Jordan.

"The guards are taken out or we get sneaky," Jordan said.

My smile indicated we were on the same page but what stunned me was that Asya was too.

"Beware of Greeks bearing gifts," she said, in a surprisingly adult voice.

Margaret and Randy

Jordan and Elizabeth mirrored my surprise though I shouldn't have been since Asya's abilities continually amazed me. I turned toward her.

"You're *really* smart! That's what we're thinking but instead of bringing a gift we'll be sending one out," I said.

"The State Department condemned King's arrest so he'll never be extradited," Jordan said.

"How long do we have?" I asked.

"Until his trial in three weeks. The verdict will take another week and then our chance is gone," Jordan said.

"Have you decided who we can use?" I asked.

"Yes, a retired Special Forces officer who's worked with the FBI to rescue hostages. He lives on a farm in Vermont and can be here tomorrow if he's interested."

"An upfront five-million-dollar payment with five-million-dollars for expenses should interest him," I said.

"We're being paid twenty-five million dollars," Jordan reminded me.

"Yes, but the company must make a small profit," I said, sweetly.

Chapter 120

I met Calvin the next day and his initial words reassured me.

"Our first move would be reconnaissance: appraising the situation and learning where the guards are at all times. We'd need a small unit acting as a team, each knowing what the others would do in a given circumstance," he said.

I nodded approval to Jordan and turned toward Calvin.

"Has Jordan described the job?" I asked.

"No. He only said that it would be a rescue which would be silently supported by the American government."

"That's true. It's the freeing of an American being held under house arrest in Venezuela. His real crime is having made a successful business deal against government officials," I said.

"Are you speaking of King?" Calvin asked.

Feeling unable to answer until he accepted the assignment, I just smiled.

"For running this operation your upfront fee will be five-million-dollars with an additional five-million-dollars for expenses. If successful, there may be similarly rewarding jobs in the future. All with the approval of a Western government since we're a law-abiding company," I said.

Margaret and Randy

I read Calvin's assent in his face and not only for the money. Angered by this disgraceful treatment of a fellow American, it didn't matter that he didn't know the victim. He would have had the same feeling if a big fellow hit his little sister, he told us later.

After receiving his bank's wiring instructions, I left the job in his hands.

Chapter 121

"What makes Calvin tick?" I asked after Calvin left.

"How do you mean?" Jordan asked.

"Mercenaries tend to be simple-minded, Not those who swagger at West Point parades but simply say, 'Pay me and I'll kill the bastards for you.' Anyone volunteering for war in a remote area of the globe has to be a bit crazy. So what makes Calvin tick?" I asked.

Jordan sipped his coffee before answering. Though being a non-coffee drinking Mormon, my office on Greenwich's waterfront contains the coffee-making machine found in the best auto dealerships. Guests and employees expect coffee and a manager's job is to please regardless of their private sentiments.

"He's a hillbilly," Jordan said finally.

Then, noting my displeasure, he asked, "*What*?"

"It's personal. When my family was poor, I wore Salvation Army clothes and he kids nicknamed me *hillbilly*. Kids can be cruel, but go on," I said.

Jordan swallowed before answering.

"Except for his temper he's a wonderful soldier, the kind you'd want covering your back. He was the ideal West Point cadet: a rookie seeking brotherhood and service and his life was that checklist: West Point, the Infantry, and the Army's elite Rangers.

"He grew up in New Hampshire and his parents divorced when he was four. His father is an accountant and his mother is a lawyer. He heard about West Point from his mother's boyfriend. The first day of high school, when the guidance counselor asked for questions, Calvin asked, 'How do I get into West Point?'"

"West Point seeks scholar-athletes with leadership potential so Calvin ran cross-country, gained A's, and was elected Student President while being just an ordinary teenager: smoking and chasing girls and getting drunk at concerts."

"Where did it go wrong?" I asked, as Calvin paused.

"I was getting there," he said, with a smile.

Chapter 122

"Calvin didn't have it," Jordan said.

"Didn't have what?" I asked.

"The most critical ability for advancement in the military."

"Which is?" I asked.

"A talent for kissing ass."

"You're kidding," I said.

"Nope. That's a quote from a four-star general whose name escapes me. Calvin didn't have it and didn't control his temper when it counted. Not that what he did doesn't stand to his credit," Jordan said.

"Just tell me what happened," I said, feeling confused.

"A mission went sideways thanks to an officer who never should have been given command. But his uncle was a senator and such things count. The order was to capture a terrorist in an Iraqi town about which little was known. Calvin and his men knew this but the colonel didn't get it.

"When the unit moved in, all hell broke loose. Three of Calvin's men were killed and four others were wounded. Things would have been worse but for Calvin's bravery, and except for one of the dead soldiers all might have been quickly forgotten. A football hero, he left a million-dollar career to join the military after the 9/11 terror attack. To avoid responsibility, the colonel placed blame for this soldier's death on Calvin, stating that he'd been ordered to reconnoiter but not to attack the town before reinforcements arrived."

"A cover-your-ass hustle," I said.

"Yes, except that when he told this to reporters, Calvin decked him. The Army might have buried the incident except that its video went viral as world-wide terrorist propaganda. *American officer attacks superior after murder of innocents*, was their theme.

"The truth couldn't drown out the video and Calvin's military career ended. He'd tormented before choosing the Infantry over gaining a civilian skill like Aviation where, after retirement, he could fly helicopters for the wealthy or FBI. He'd prayed before deciding, asking himself how much he would sacrifice if he chose Infantry over Aviation and for God to pick his branch. He finally chose Infantry, never having wanted to do anything but serve his country.

"So when he was chucked from the Army, the only marketable skill he had to support his family was as a soldier for private military contractors," Jordan concluded.

The memory of a similar event hit me. A feisty New York City Police officer was blackballed for slugging a reporter who had grabbed her ass as cameras rolled. We met on a plane to Berlin, I to visit my father, Vladimir, and she to lick her wounds with relatives. I suggested that she talk to Vladimir and he quickly hired her, becoming one of our company's most valuable employees.

Margaret and Randy

"The path to one's true vocation can be surprising. Calvin is our kind of guy," I said, with barely a moment's deliberation.

Margaret and Randy

Chapter 123

Calvin's plan wasn't original. Long before, Libyan terrorists smuggled guns into Britain similarly and a closely shadowed British spy, Oleg Gordievsky, was smuggled from Russia via Finland in the trunk of a car to meet a hero's welcome in London. Once, a newly deposed Nigerian president was drugged, blindfolded, and locked in a wooden crate labeled "EXTRA CARGO" but been discovered and released by customs officials before leaving the London airport.

Still, what counted was that Calvin's plan worked. The house's large grand piano was crated for shipment to a friendly diplomat in Norway. During a refueling stop, King was freed from the container and placed on a private plane bound for home. Doubtless, the diplomat enjoys his new musical instrument.

Venezuela protested as the world applauded. Not that mega-financiers are popular but because the benefits of a just legal system are understood.

Two weeks later, as the children were sleeping, I relaxed beside Randy in bed.

"It worked out with King," he said, matter-of-factly.

"Thankfully, though it was a tricky operation with one step after another balanced on a hairspring," I said.

Margaret and Randy

"Was there a back-up plan? If King was discovered at the airport?" he asked.

"There was. The airport is on the water. Calvin had four retired SEALS ready to grab King and put him onto a speedboat bound for Columbia from where he would be flown home."

"It's good that wasn't needed," Randy said.

"None of us wanted a shootout," I agreed.

I frowned as the gravity of my statement hit me, luck and the fragility of life. Randy sensed my distress.

"You need a vacation," he said, with concern.

"We both do," I said, clasping my hands over my belly, with the smile that only a woman can give.

His bafflement turned to a knowing grin as he grasped my meaning.

"In seven months and not twins this time. Our long road together has sometimes been hard but splendid too. Though not the usual path, I wouldn't change it for all that I've read in the romances," I said.

"Nor would I, my love. Nor would I." Randy said, placing his hands over mine.

www.ingramcontent.com/pod-product-compliance
Lightning Source LLC
Chambersburg PA
CBHW020442270626
47155CB00022B/933